THE
LOST PAGES

R.D. FRANCIS

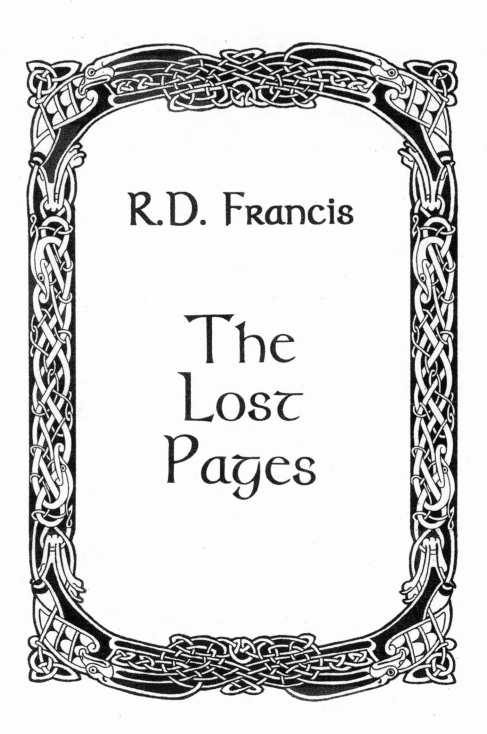

R.D. Francis

The Lost Pages

To order additional copies of this book, contact:
Xlibris LLC
1-800-455-039
www.xlibris.com.au
Orders@xlibris.com.au
513273

CONTENTS

British Iles

Iona ●

Scotland

† Lindisfarne
●

†

Ireland

† †
† Kells
● †
† †
● Dublin

† †

Anglesey

†

St. Asaph
●

England

Wales

Monasteries †

Hereford ●

Oxford ●

Devizes
Bristol ●
Bath ● Market London ●
Lavington
Imber

Isles
of Scilly

INTRODUCTION

Jack Harrison is settled into a successful career in the Secret Service but it abruptly changes when he is almost killed and his engagement breaks up because of his difficult lifestyle.

He decides that there must be a better way and decides to go as far away as he can to continue his artistic interest in Ancient History, Manuscripts and Calligraphy.

He buys a small hobby farm in Tasmania, Australia where he is happy for two years . . . but then his life changes surprisingly again.

To Frank & Janet Scrivener
for being a good friend.
from Roger D. Francis
x
& June Francis (DESIGNER)
X.

PREFACE

F ather Bernard rose early that morning with a light heart and a sense of anticipation, because today was to be his last day on the much loved manuscript he had been working on for so long. His dormitory, like those of all the other brothers at the monastery, was situated above the monks' parlour. He moved silently down the stone stairs, along the cold passage to the Warming House, where he hoped to get his old bones warm and his circulation going by rubbing his hands together vigorously.

It had been another frosty midwinter's night, but his fingers needed to be flexible to complete his writing for the last time. This work was important to him. He was dedicated to his task, and also to his good long-time friend, the Abbott of Kells, who had asked him to stay on past retirement from the scriptorium, to pass his skills on to those of the younger scribes who showed the most calligraphic promise.

His hands were warmer now, so he went into the kitchen and being early, was the first to be served. Father Bernard walked into the refectory where he was soon joined by the other brothers. He ate and drank quickly of the freshly baked bread, honey, ale and warm goat's milk, all prepared by the brothers of the Abbey. His young apprentice Peter sat down with him. Father Bernard had chosen his successor with care, because the future of the scriptorium now lay in his younger, skilful hands.

The Monastery of Kells was very self-sufficient and excelled in animal husbandry and farming, keeping the brothers well supplied with vegetables of every kind, meat, honey, wheat and fish. The animals also supplied the calf, sheep or goat skins that were so essential for the scriptorium; they provided vellum for the making of manuscripts.

Father Bernard and Peter spoke quietly, planning the day's work ahead. What they would finish was to prove to be a masterpiece, but to them and the other brothers in Kells, it was just a part of their ongoing dedication.

Father Bernard said, 'Will you please go first to the room and light the fire, Peter?' Even though the scriptorium, with its small diamond-shaped windows, was one of the first rooms in the monastery to be glazed, the room was still very cold. Peter soon had the fire blazing away merrily and it was a very welcoming sight by the time Father Bernard reached the room from the Chapter House.

Peter had learned the skill of quill cutting from his mentor and now brought out some new pens he had cut earlier. Peter studied the prepared vellum which had been made for today's work, to be sure that the surface was correct. He then started to prepare the inks and colours that would be needed to start the pages, testing them all on scraps of vellum. Peter particularly loved the beautiful blue which he made with the ground *Lapis lazuli*, a semi-precious stone from far-away Afghanistan. He wondered what it would be like if he could visit some of the far-away places he knew only by name.

Father Bernard had already planned the page, but now he studied it one last time before starting, to ensure that the limner had correctly marked, with his hard, fine, metal point, the faint indentations of lines that would be a guide for the lettering.

The morning sun from the east burst from behind the clouds over the snow-capped hillsides, filling the scriptorium with light. Concentrating intensely, both men began to write.

SURPRISE VISITOR

The wretched phone started ringing as I put the old Holden Ute away in my new barn. I could just hear the phone's persistent ringing, being carried on the afternoon sea breeze past the farmhouse. This was the third day it had rung at an awkward time and it was beginning to irritate me.

I muttered an ugly word under my breath and let it ring. My number was unlisted and I had been careful to only give the number to close friends or farming equipment and foodstuff suppliers. It was possibly a wrong number but what fool would keep ringing a wrong number? My friends knew I couldn't or wouldn't answer until after six o'clock. So who was the mystery caller?

I was debating whether to unload the timber and fencing equipment out of the Ute when I realised the ringing had finally stopped. When I bought the farm from the previous owners they were happy to include the Ute, as it's commonly known in Australia, in the price. The local garage gave it a full service, a new battery and it hadn't missed a beat since. It was considered the farmers' everyday workhorse. My new neighbour Peter Morris, who lived on the other side of the valley, had given me plenty of good advice as to where to have it serviced and also given me one of his cattle dogs called Nick.

Nick, who was now looking up at me, expecting an order or a word of encouragement, was now about five years old and knew everything a cattle dog should know about contrary sheep and lumbering cattle. Peter said the dog knew more about farming than I did and therefore we would get on well. He made that remark about two years ago, but I now believe he wasn't far off the truth.

The summer had been glorious; indeed it had been like one of the summers that I had yearned for as a young boy in England. No doubt the friends I had left behind in the northern hemisphere would envy my good fortune. They by now, it being early April, were hoping for an early spring with rain. My local farming friends in Tasmania, on the other hand, were looking forward to a mild winter again with some decent rain to fill the farm dams.

Occasionally a morning winter frost would surprise us, but we were quite near the Derwent Estuary and the mid-morning sun had enough warmth so that the frost soon vanished. I loved the eucalyptus trees because they didn't drop their leaves all at once in autumn like deciduous trees, and the air had a special clarity and freshness that enabled you to see enormous distances.

These factors and a few other things finally clinched my decision to settle down here and make a new life in Tasmania, but not to retire. I wasn't quite thirty and I had seen much of the world and experienced a lot of excitement – too much excitement at times, working for British Government Intelligence. The Department had received a lot of bad press lately. Typically, if you got into trouble in a foreign country the government didn't want to acknowledge your existence.

At first I thought the remuneration was good, but later, in a moment of reflection I remembered that I almost lost the sight in one eye, and if I had been much closer to the bomb in the Middle East, I might have been killed. As it was, my hearing was slightly impaired. That time I was lucky, but next time, who knows? I could be unlucky.

Danger is a stimulant so they say, but I thought I'd had enough to last me a long time. I wanted to revive my tortured body and spirit. In my schooldays I had been a keen sportsman and in good shape, which was one of the reasons why I was able to get the job in intelligence combined with my academic qualifications.

By now it was mid afternoon and I had finished work early because it was Thursday, my usual day for going into Hobart to my evening class in calligraphy. I was looking forward to rejoining the class and increasing my knowledge of this most noble of ancient arts.

I didn't want to be late. Tonight was the first night of the new term. After a quick shower and shave, I changed into more suitable clothing. I took a beer out of the fridge and sat down to relax in my usual comfortable chair on the veranda that gave me a commanding view of the scenery. From this position I could see it all – the river below me flowing into the estuary, which in turn flowed past almost deserted beaches on its way to the sea. In the extreme distance I could just see the hazy blue outline of Mt Wellington rising above the city of Hobart. I also enjoyed watching the magnificent wedge-tailed eagles from this position as they circled high above on the thermal currents of air, gliding majestically above me; which gave me endless pleasure. The fine group of tall trees on my land was perfect for them to nest in, so I felt satisfied that these magnificent birds were safe on my hobby farm.

Having woken early at six that morning, as I usually did to get through the work that is the daily lot of farmers everywhere, I mentally checked the tasks I had set myself this morning and felt very satisfied with the day's results.

As I turned slightly in the chair to get up and make something to eat before leaving, I caught a glint of sunlight reflected from a car windscreen. It aroused my curiosity and so I watched the small blue car driving along the road on the other side of the valley. I had made a few good friends since my arrival, but this was an unknown car to me. Whoever it was, was driving very slowly along the dirt road and picking their way carefully to avoid the potholes. Definitely a stranger, I confirmed, because most of my farming friends wouldn't have cared a damn about potholes.

It wasn't the local church minister either, who would drop in occasionally with his wife for a glass of sherry, a chinwag and a most enjoyable evening. Any interruptions to my plans for this evening were, to say the least, inconvenient. The minister would understand my eagerness to leave. I never explained to this charming man what my previous occupation had been, but if I had I am sure he would have been horrified. The car disappeared from view briefly, as it made its way across the lush fertile valley and over the timber bridge that spanned the stream. The car was obviously coming to my farm, but I couldn't think why. Perhaps the driver was lost and wanted directions. So I waited, curious.

At first I could just see the top of the car, but then the front of the car rose up as it came onto the level track before the top gate. The car stopped and a tall figure got out and struggled with the gate. He was surely no local farmer, I thought. Then I realised who it was. I leaped up from my comfortable chair, ran inside and grabbed the binoculars. As I focused them, I knew my guess had been right: it was B.J. Loader, my old boss from the Intelligence Department in London. This could only mean trouble for me.

What the hell is he doing out here so far from London? I wondered, muttering under my breath.

I was never too sure about Loader. He just didn't suit me, and I knew he felt the same way about me; he could also be most irritable at times. The forthcoming conversation was not going to be easy.

He struggled to close the top gate and then got back in the car. The engine roared into life again, lurched forward and the engine stalled. That wouldn't make his temper any better. I stayed in my chair and finished off the bottle of beer, remaining seated as his car drove up in front of the veranda. He was not getting a rapturous welcome from me. What the hell could he possibly want? I was feeling decidedly uneasy.

He got out of the car carefully and slowly approached, adjusting his expensive Savile Row suit as he did so. As he came closer, it was obvious he was not quite sure how to start the conversation. We looked at each other. Finally he said, 'May I sit down? I have an interesting proposal which you might like.'

An original conversation opener, I mused. In the past his attitude and bearing would be very much different. He would be tearing shreds off me for not following correct procedures and my incomplete reports were a nuisance to him. Generally I played the game my way. Paper pusher I definitely was not.

To call our business a game was a lie of course – dirty tricks department was nearer to the truth. I studied him carefully and noted he had put on a bit of weight; he was puffing a little and his complexion was flushed. I was keen to ask him what he was doing in my secluded part of the world, but didn't.

'We haven't seen each other for a couple of years, Harrison,' he said slowly. 'I must say you look very fit and healthy. Are you still practising martial arts and boxing?'

I assured him that I was. 'But you are intruding into my peaceful life, which I now cherish very much.'

He stopped still and looked around the garden pretending to admire my fledgling rose garden. He and I had only one thing in common, and that was a love of roses. However, I didn't wish to encourage that line of conversation. He was going to make me late for my evening class. Finally, I broke the silence.

'You had better come inside,' I said tersely, 'and tell me what all this is about. You are a hell of a long way from London for a fireside chat, so it must be important.' I opened the door and followed him inside to the lounge.

'I have a project for you,' he said, as he made his way to the nearest armchair. 'I think you would find it interesting.'

'I guessed as much,' I replied cautiously. I tried to slow him down a bit and went into the kitchen to make a pot of tea. 'Hold on, I'm making some tea, but I can't stop long because I have an appointment in Hobart tonight.

'You're right. We haven't got much time, I'm afraid,' he replied quickly.

The slightly anxious tone in his voice made me put down the tea caddy. I looked around the corner into the lounge. He had taken off his topcoat and was laying it carefully on the back of the chair. I looked again around the corner into the lounge. The meticulously dressed Loader was fidgeting and looking admiringly around the room at the paintings and calligraphy works of mine and my fellow artists on the walls.

'What's this thing?' he said, pointing at the woodheater.

'Oh, they're great. They come in very useful in winter. Log fires are very popular here, especially if you have your own farm or land, you've got your own fuel. It keeps me very fit also, chopping and sawing logs for firewood.'

'So I see,' he grunted. 'How's the tea going?'

'Fine, just fine, sit down and relax. The tea won't be long,' I replied.

I went back into the kitchen, finished making the tea, cut several slices of fruit cake the minister's wife had kindly made for me, and put them on a plate. I placed the whole lot on a tray and carried it into the lounge and set it down on the low table between the two comfortable armchairs.

'This is most civilised,' he said, obviously trying to be complimentary.

'Of course,' I replied bluntly. 'Now come on. I have to go to Hobart tonight.'

'For your calligraphy night class at 7:30 pm,' he replied firmly. 'Jack, since settling down here, you have revived a run down farm – congratulations by the way – and taken up other interests, which I'll refer to later.'

I knew what he was referring to when he mentioned my other interests, but I let him carry on. I was intrigued to know what else he knew about my life in Tasmania.

'You've become a man of letters,' he said with a slight hint of humour in his voice as he munched the cake ravenously.

I almost laughed. 'That's stretching it a bit far, but . . .'

He suddenly stopped me with a wave of his hand and remained poised and then, as if remembering something, he said, 'I would like to see one of your famous beaches.'

'What about your tea?' I protested. 'You've hardly touched it.'

'Never mind, we can always have another later,' he said firmly.

He seemed so insistent that I let him have his way and we went out to the barn and got into my Land Rover. I casually jumped into the driver's seat while he struggled in the other side.

'Having trouble?' I smiled. He shook his head but said nothing. I thought perhaps he was in pain, or maybe he was thinking how he could persuade me to take on this unknown project. As we travelled along my bush track he remained silent, obviously thinking, and all my attempts at conversation were unsuccessful. I was concerned about my evening class, which I looked as if I was going to miss, or at least be very late.

When we came off the bush track on to the sealed road and turned towards our small town, I took my eyes off the road momentarily to study his face: he was tight lipped and staring blankly into the foot well. We reached my favourite beach in about ten or twelve minutes and I drove over to some pine trees that had been planted to act as a windbreak and to provide shade for picnickers. From this vantage point we could see the beach, the sand dunes and the headland at the far end of the bay. The afternoon sea breeze had now started to gently blow in from the sea and cool our faces.

The scene before us was magnificent. Surely, I thought, he would understand why I preferred my new life here. He got out of the Land Rover and slowly walked into the sunshine, obviously expecting me to follow. I did so and as I joined him, waiting for him to say something, I said, 'What do you think of the view?'

He appeared to be lost for the right word and then he said, 'Beautiful, Jack. Beautiful.' He shook his head as if clearing his mind. 'But this isn't why I came here and sought you out.'

'Thought not,' I said. 'Perhaps you had better enlighten me.'

Then he said something that brought me back to reality. 'Have you had trouble with your phone in the last day or two?' he asked, almost casually.

I didn't have to think about that. My answer was, 'Yes, but it is fine now.'

'Of course it's working fine,' he growled. 'They've probably bugged you. Where were you when they came to repair the so-called fault?'

'Where do you think,' I said angrily. 'I'm a working farmer now. I was in the new barn – working. They were there for less than half an hour.'

He grunted. 'Hell! That means that they believe that you could be involved or they're just taking out insurance in case you are. That's the reason we had to get out of the house.'

Loader was now starting to annoy me by not coming to the point – and making me late.

'Who the hell are "they", anyway?' I said, emphasising the word 'they'. 'Could they perhaps be the Mafia, IRA or some dishonest billionaire with his own private army of thugs?' I said.

'I'm not sure,' he said reflectively. 'It could be all of them, or just one of them, but the most likely candidate of course would be the IRA.'

'Why "of course" the IRA? I know absolutely zero about this and you've told me nothing so far. Start making sense Loader!'

He didn't answer my question. 'You should not have let the pseudo phone men into your house anyway,' he grumbled.

'Why not?' I replied angrily, 'I'm out of your world now and not a 'company' man anymore.'

'Once a company man, always a company man,' he muttered tersely. 'You should know that a field intelligence officer never really retires.'

'All right, put me in the picture, but quickly. Although I am not saying I'll help. I would rather stay here and continue doing what I've always wanted to do.'

Loader turned and walked toward the picnic table under the trees and sat down. 'What I am getting at is this: You were always interested in old books, religious history, old maps and generally a bit of a scholar. You were a damn rebel and probably still are. Am I right? You were very keen on calligraphy too.'

I sat down at the other side of the table, rather flattered at his appraisal of my interests, but wary of his remarks.

'Yes, I suppose so,' I said cautiously. 'But how did you know all this?' I continued. 'Sorry – that was a damn silly question to ask you, of course.'

'Yes,' he said with a slight smile. 'My question to you now, is this – can you tell the difference between one calligraphic style and another?'

'Yes, I certainly can, well most of the major ones I think. There are so many – but what the hell is all this to do with you? It's my hobby now, simply that. I have practised it for pure enjoyment and nothing more, studying it now for five terms since retiring to Tasmania to further my knowledge'

'Long enough I would have thought,' he answered quickly. 'Have you heard of Edward Johnston. Or the *Lindisfarne Gospels*? The *Book of Durrow*? Or indeed – the *Book of Kells*? Which is a priceless manuscript – possibly from the 8th century?'

At this point I swung around to face him. 'Yes, of course I have! Edward Johnston is widely credited with reviving the lost art of calligraphy in Britain and the *Book of Kells* is in the Library of Trinity College, Dublin. And so is the *Book of Durrow*. The *Lindisfarne Gospels*, however, are in the British Library, London. I know that because I have seen it several times, in my spare moments from the office.'

'Ah, good,' he said with a smile. 'Your teacher has done an excellent job. I would like to meet him someday.'

'You can't,' I said swiftly,' because he's a lady.'

'Oh really! Very interesting. Is she young and pretty? If so, I can understand your interest in the classes then,' he said with a sarcastic tone in his voice.

'Cut it out, Loader! Get to the damn point.' He had touched a raw nerve with me because of my previous failed engagement.

'Have you seen the *Book of Kells*?' he continued, totally unaffected by my outburst.

'No, unfortunately. Not the original at least, only full colour plates in books. There are many books published with excellent reproductions in them, but one day I hope to go to Dublin to see the real thing.'

He gave a crafty smile. 'Your luck is about to change old friend,' he chuckled. 'Tell me, would you be able to detect the difference between a page from the *Book of Kells* and a page from the *Lindisfarne Gospels*?'

I considered the question much more carefully this time. 'I'm not sure; they are both magnificent and written in a similar Insular Half-Uncial style at about the same time – well, within a few years of one another. I believe – perhaps I can.'

'I'm most impressed with your knowledge, Jack,' he said quietly, this time without any sarcasm.

However, I was unimpressed by his flattery. 'I have several books back at the farm, which would help us, but before we go any further would you please explain what this is all about?' I was getting very concerned about missing my evening class.

In response he carefully took a small flat box out of the side pocket of his overcoat. In the box was a folder which he passed to me. I opened it very carefully and inside was a photograph wrapped in cotton and silk, just a bit larger than the palm of my hand.

What it showed quite clearly was a page from a medieval book written in Latin in an Insular Uncial style. I was surprised and wondered where it had come from. The corners of the photograph were slightly the worse for wear and faded. It was a sepia print, but still clear enough to see, which dated the photograph from about the first half of the twentieth century, I estimated. But no more information could I find.

Loader could see that I was very interested. 'Well, what do you think?' he said. 'Intriguing, isn't it?' He was studying my face very carefully.

I had to agree, because it held my utmost attention. 'Where's it come from?' I said.

'That's part of the puzzle. Someone came across it by chance in an antique shop somewhere in the County of Wiltshire, north of Stonehenge. Unfortunately the trail ran cold because it came from a deceased estate and the old antique dealer couldn't remember which one, or how long it had been in his shop. Tragic luck then followed – the eminent customer who found it was killed in a suspicious, strange and horrific car accident on his way to a second meeting with his long-standing friend, who happened to be the top expert from the Bodleian Library in Oxford. A man with an extensive knowledge of medieval documents.'

'End of story then,' I said rather sorrowfully. 'What was the result?' I said, trying to sound concerned.

'This you wouldn't believe,' he said quietly. By now I thought I had been patient long enough, because he had been playing me like a skilful angler tempts a trout. And now he had me on the hook. 'The photograph,' he continued, 'was taken between the first and second world wars, in the mid to late 1930s. It's a good photo, taken by a keen amateur, of one of the missing pages of the *Book of Kells*. We're quite sure of it.'

'Surely that's not possible,' I interjected. 'The book is complete – isn't it?'

'No, apparently not. You see, over the many centuries the book has been rebound several times. I haven't got all the information, but you can find that out yourself. Human beings are not always honest – if a page or pages were damaged by a bookbinder, then perhaps that page wasn't included in the rebinding. The book has had an extremely hard life. It was rebound rather badly in early Victorian times by trimming the edges, and remarkably, it was never quite finished by the original artists.'

'That's understandable. And extraordinary,' I said. 'But how do you know the photo was taken by a very keen amateur?'

'It's an excellent photo and the size indicates it was taken on a small plate camera and not your small inexpensive family 'Box Brownie' size. However, a true professional would have used a much bigger format and stamped their name on the back or front – at least that's our photographic team's expert opinion.'

'I would agree. That all seems to make sense. But tell me, there's something else that's puzzling me. How is it you are here in Australia for such a relatively minor matter?'

'I was coming to Australia for a high level meeting with our Australian ASIO counterpart. It so happened that this matter came up in Cabinet before I left and – in spite of what you think – this is extremely important. The Cabinet and the Prime Minister discussed this at length with me. The PM himself insisted that you were asked first.'

I almost laughed. 'Now you are kidding,' I said. 'The PM doesn't even know me.'

'Partially true,' he said. 'But he does know your father very well. Have you forgotten that the PM and your father were close colleagues when they were lowly backbenchers about twenty years ago? Things have changed dramatically since then.' He continued, 'Both of them were eager young politicians with a burning desire to be of some use to their country.' He nodded and smiled.

'That's true,' I replied cautiously. 'But I still don't think I am the man you want. What about Fisher or Bennett – can't you persuade them? They're both good experienced agents.'

'They are both non-starters I'm afraid. Fisher is in hospital with both legs mending well, but not quickly enough, and Bennett is fully occupied in what we used to call Yugoslavia. Besides, no-one has your extensive knowledge about this particular subject and that gives you the vital edge.'

I desperately tried to think of someone else who might be suitable but couldn't. They were either too old or inexperienced, or would be unsuitable because it was not their sphere of interest. So I gave up. I considered his last remark about my knowledge of this particular subject and realised it was perhaps a rather strange hobby for me as an intelligence agent.

'Thanks for the vote of confidence.' I said. How was I to manage with the farm and I wondered how – or indeed, if – I could get someone in and for how long. 'All right, let's say I'm interested. How long before I get a positive result and what about the financial reward? If I can get someone to look after the farm they'll need to be paid too.'

'I'm empowered to offer you a hundred thousand pounds plus expenses!' he said with a pained look on his face, as if the money was coming from his own pocket. 'Plus expenses,' he emphasised again. 'As soon as you agree, the money will be in your account! And I did say pounds not dollars!'

The amount was very tempting. This must be a serious business showing how desperate he was. Then he finished by saying:' I think it would take about a month approximately depending how you progress.'

'Good grief, are you serious?' I glanced at him again, as if for confirmation and he wasn't joking. 'All right, I can see that this is important to you, so I'll have a word with one of my farming friends and see if it's possible. But I'm still not keen to get involved in your vulgar world of espionage and violence again. That's why I came here to make a fresh start in my own way.'

He nodded his head as if understanding. 'I appreciate what you are saying, Jack. But let me know damn quickly. Time is pressing. It's essential we get those lost pages first. Coming second is no damn use to us at all – we would still be the loser.'

We strode quickly to the Land Rover and I drove back to the farm, both of us saying very little. I had plenty to think about and plan, and he was probably worrying whether he had made the right choice in asking me.

Loader handed me an envelope and said, 'Here is some further important information, details and contacts you will find useful. Keep it safe.' As we got out of the Land Rover I put the envelope into the glove box and locked it for safe keeping.

It would be getting dark in a couple of hours and I had started work soon after six that morning, so it had been a long day and there was still much to do. Loader was pressing me for a quick decision. I made him comfortable and showed him where everything was so that he could make tea or coffee, or a simple meal if he wished.

If there was anyone I could trust to look after the farm there could only be one choice and that was Peter Morris, who had a property on the other side of our small town. Peter was a typical Australian farmer who could turn his hand to most things on the farm, mend things and build barns or sheds that wouldn't blow down in a gale.

He was tall, tanned and tough. When he helped me get things repaired, I struggled physically at first to keep up with him. He had also been a tremendous source of knowledge on local country matters, which was of immense help. You could not help liking him; he was the sort you could rely on in a tough situation.

My first task now was to persuade him to look after the farm, which was a tall order. Although I trusted him, I obviously didn't want to tell him the real reason for my request, which seemed unfair to him after everything he had done to get me back on my feet and the farm into good working order. I did not see any point in explaining to him.

By the time I had reached Peter's farm I had decided to tell him that my father's solicitor had called from London concerning some important family matters about property and that he needed my help. I was no actor but I hoped I could sound convincing. As I approached their farm buildings, Peter's wife Kathy greeted me cordially from the front veranda.

I envied Peter because he and Kathy worked together like a team. Both of them seemed to know what to do in any situation and nothing seemed to faze them. They had a couple of young boys who liked me from the moment we met and were soon calling me 'Uncle' or 'Jack'. I wondered sadly if I should ever be so lucky. In life of course luck didn't really come into it. It was all hard work.

'Hi, how are you Jack?' Kathy called. 'Come on in. Peter is in the shower. He's finished for the day.'

'I'm afraid I have a favour to ask you both but I should wait until Peter's finished and talk to you together,' I replied.

'Come on,' she said, 'don't look so concerned. Take a seat in the lounge Jack, Peter won't be much longer.'

Peter finished and came in rubbing his hair. 'Well, how can we help?'

He grinned and sat down opposite me. 'Farming problem or an affair of the heart?' Peter occasionally teased me about my love life, or lack of it, but it was all in good-natured fun, so I didn't take offence.

'Neither. I'm sorry – no third guess, Peter. My father needs my help with some large land property transactions and, as he hasn't been too well lately, his solicitor rang me and suggested that I was needed. It's a big favour to ask, but can you keep an eye on the farm? I can pay one of the men to work for me, if you can oversee things?'

Kathy looked at Peter and nodded. He smiled and said, 'That's no problem, but for how long?'

I hesitated. 'I can't be sure, probably about a month. It's a wild guess.'

'That's fine. Leave it to us,' he said calmly. 'I know pretty well what's needed on your farm,' he smiled and laughed, 'and of course, so does Nick.'

Inwardly I breathed a sigh of relief and, with that settled in my mind, I felt much better, although I didn't like telling them a white lie. The real reason of course would take too long and encourage too many questions that I couldn't answer anyway. They kindly offered me a solid meal before I went, but I managed to excuse myself without being abrupt, explaining that I had many arrangements to make before leaving. I was hoping, if I was successful in my quest, that I could tell them the truth, or at least as much as I was able one day. Little did I know what was ahead of me!

A NASTY SHOCK

As I drove back it was late afternoon and the summer sun was making its way toward Mt Wellington as it had done for millions of years. I started to think of Loader and whether he would like something to drink – beer, wine or spirits. He was a wine drinker I remembered. Should I buy something at the local bottle shop?

My attention was distracted by a dark limousine travelling at high speed towards me, clipping the dirt edge of the road as it poured on the power. It passed at well over the speed limit and I could just discern three dark figures inside. Although I didn't get the number plate, I noticed a prominent hire car sticker on the back window. I drove on through the town at an increasing speed. Something was not quite as it should be; I had that little niggling feeling of unease that you get sometimes.

As I approached the farm I noticed that the bottom gate was open. That concerned me, because I was certain I had closed it properly. Ramming my foot hard down on the throttle I approached the top gate and saw that it too was swinging in the breeze. The feeling of unease grew as I pushed the Land Rover harder, as it bumped and lurched.

I could see Loader's car, which for some reason was sitting there where he had left it – but now with the driver's door ajar, the key in the ignition and the instrument panel lights on. I switched everything off and locked the door; something strange had happened I realised.

The tight feeling in my chest and the adrenalin pumping around my head didn't help me think clearly. Rushing into the house to find him brought another nasty shock. The place was a mess. Books, papers, discs and tapes were strewn everywhere. Furniture had been moved; the pictures on the wall were crooked. They had also been through my writing bureau, my calligraphy light desk; plus the computer had been left on. Going from room to room the result was the same – total chaos, but still no sign of Loader. I began to fear for his safety as I rushed outside again.

The three characters in the dark limousine I had seen driving back in the direction of Hobart were obviously the prime suspects. Searching for him in the fading light and shouting frantically, I stopped occasionally in the hope of a reply, but grim silence was all that returned.

I raced round the corner of the new barn and noticed the cattle in the pen were very distressed and breathing heavily, they were covered in muck and the ground was well churned up. I glimpsed a huddled figure over in the far corner under the lowest horizontal bar. It had to be Loader. He was a sorry mess, his expensive grey suit ruined. He lay very still and did not seem to be breathing and, as I approached him, it was obvious several cattle had trampled on him. His mouth, nose and ear were bleeding and he had a nasty cut across the forehead. I had to do something quickly. I checked his pulse at the neck. Much to my surprise there was a faint but rapid pulse. He opened his eyes slowly and tried to speak and then passed out again. I suspected his jaw was broken too. While he was unconscious I checked his pockets and everything was intact – wallet and passport – so they were not after money, just information I realised.

Making him as comfortable as possible by dragging him slowly out of the pen I quickly got the cattle to the other side of the pen and rang for an ambulance. Returning to him in the twilight, I covered him with a foil blanket that I had used for bushwalking then wiped his face with a damp cloth. When a man's life is in danger and you're the only one there, it's difficult to know which problem to tackle first. I checked his mouth for blood and vomit, taking care not to move his head. Sitting with him quietly, I contemplated the bizarre happenings of the day and with regret that my peaceful way of life had certainly ended, at least for a while.

Loader moved slightly and with immense difficulty murmured, 'Get those pages Jack.' Although I only heard the word 'pages' clearly, it was enough for me to understand him.

'Don't talk or move,' I whispered back. 'The ambulance will be here any minute. How many were there?' I asked.

He held up his left hand and with pain written in his face managed to show me three fingers.

'What did they look like – Mediterranean type, Oriental or Anglo-Saxon?' I felt awkward asking him, but I had to know, before he passed out again.

He struggled once more and mouthed the word 'one', so at least I knew what or whom I was expecting. Every time he seemed to come to, I spoke to him calmly and reassured him that he would be all right. They would almost certainly be Mediterranean, probably Italian, and there were three of them.

The ambulance came in less than twenty minutes and I tried to impress upon Loader that what had happened to him was just a farming accident, nothing more, so when the ambulance officer spoke to me I explained to him that Loader was a 'city' friend who had no idea how dangerous a farm can be.

The ambulance officer said, 'I will have to report an accident of this kind to the local police. Sorry sir, so you will be hearing from them very soon.' The local police when they arrived later, asked me much the same questions and seemed satisfied with my fake analysis. They said a few words of sympathy and made a note or two and then left.

As the ambulance officers made Loader comfortable to go into the Royal Hobart Hospital, I quietly spoke to him again and assured him that I would take on the project, and not to worry. He managed a painful faint smile, but with great difficulty. Hardly surprising, considering the shocking condition he was in. Loader was just conscious enough to understand what I was saying.

He had risen through the ranks in our business and knew how to wriggle out of tight situations, but being confronted by three thugs probably twenty years his junior was too much for him to cope with. Although I realised he had fooled them somehow and managed to survive and pass on sufficient information to me. Thankfully he was still alive.

Now that he was in safe hands, although it would be a while before he could return to London, I started to consider my task ahead. First, I put the Land Rover in the barn next to the other farming equipment, leaving the key in the ignition for Peter to use the vehicle as necessary. As I looked around, I remembered the envelope in the glove box that Loader had given me. Opening it, I realised it contained further information that Loader had brought. He must have felt extremely confident to have it on his person so openly. Perhaps over confident, I thought. This was obviously what the trio in the flash limousine had been after. Unknown to me, the information was with me all the time while they had been giving Loader such a vicious beating.

I returned to the house and angrily looked at the mess they had left and as I cleared up, putting everything approximately in place, I checked as best I could to see if anything was missing, but everything seemed to be present and correct.

Time was not a commodity I had plenty of, so I took Loader's envelope into the kitchen and put the kettle on to make a much needed cup of tea. While it boiled, I carefully spread the information out on the round kitchen table and started reading his brief notes and suggestions.

His advice seemed to be to go to the Vatican Library in Rome first, and then Florence, and finally Venice. It included names and addresses and introductions to eminent scholars at these places, with the excellent idea of gaining a greater knowledge of the history of writing, decoration and gold illumination. Some of the notes were not his, because I knew his writing was an almost illegible scrawl. They were not signed, but were written in a confident flowing Italic script on fine quality paper. The handwriting was something to be envied, but as it was not signed it didn't help a great deal.

One other memorandum, however, that held my attention read:

> Loader – Most urgent we get these pages before anyone else. I wish to present them to the Irish Government as part of the goodwill process.

The Prime Minister had signed it, so that was why this quest was so important. I didn't know the Prime Minister's writing well of course. I suspect very few did, but now it was all beginning to make sense. I read it again and, although it seemed a shame, I screwed the paper into a ball and threw it into the dying embers of the wood fire and watched it burst into flames and disappear.

Although Loader apparently thought highly of my calligraphic knowledge, I was beginning to have doubts myself, as the full enormity of the situation began to unfold. For reassurance, I returned to the lounge to find a book that would clarify, or at least strengthen, my knowledge of the subject. But I couldn't find the one book that I prized the most. It was not a 'how-to-do-it' book, but a concise book on the *History of Writing* with clear colour illustrations throughout, with particular emphasis on the *Book of Kells* and the *Lindisfarne Gospels*. Earlier that evening I had put the books away in a tremendous rush and in no particular order, but now it seemed to have gone. I checked again more thoroughly, but no luck. Regretfully I realised the thugs – who possibly might have some basic knowledge – had stolen it. The grotesqueness of the situation was suddenly highlighted and did not amuse me.

Eventually, as tiredness overcame me, I struggled into bed and slept very restlessly, tossing and turning, my mind unable to switch off. I was glad when dawn finally broke and the early morning sun shone into my bedroom.

I needed to move as quickly as possible. I showered, got dressed, grabbed a piece of fruit and plenty of cereal, with a strong cup of tea, before starting to pack. By then I was feeling much better. It was still too early to ring the travel agent, so I continued with my packing.

My choice was the biggest backpack that could be carried on the plane as hand luggage. I did not relish waiting around airports for my baggage; that was out of the question. Travel light, travel fast, I thought. I did, however, take my small digital camera for making a record of what I hopefully would find. After all, I was going supposedly as a tourist around Europe, so that would help me blend in with the crowd.

Time seemed to drag so I switched on the television. I was able to catch the last part of the news, but all it seemed to be was the usual murder, riots, flood, fire, and minor wars breaking out around the world. I turned it off in disgust after the weather forecast, which was fine weather for all the East coast of Australia. I wondered what the weather was like in Europe, particularly in Italy. Focusing my mind back on the quest, I peeped inside Loader's envelope again. There were several letters introducing me to various eminent people in Oxford, Rome, London, Venice, and Florence; but also in the bottom of the envelope was a new passport with my photo in it. Curiously I looked at the name Richard Anthony Davies. It was a photo of me taken before I left Loader's section over two years ago. The cunning old fox had been thinking ahead once again. He must have had supreme confidence that at some future date I would recover from my injuries and rejoin his section.

I checked the telephone, fax and answering machine thoroughly for listening devices and Loader was right. I had been bugged, but fortunately none of my conversations had anything to do with the matter that was now completely filling my mind. I carefully removed the listening device by placing a paperweight in the cradle as I slid the handpiece out.

It was now almost nine o'clock and feeling more hopeful, I rang my usual travel agent. A friendly voice answered.

'How can I help you, Mr Harrison?' she said, recognising my voice almost immediately. I hadn't lost my English accent and I was a good customer, flying a couple of times to Melbourne and Sydney and once to Christchurch, New Zealand for calligraphy workshops.

'Well Rachel, I have a problem. Could you book a flight for today to Rome in the name of Richard Anthony Davies?'

'Today, that's a tough one!' she responded. 'Can you leave it with me for a few minutes and I will ring you back?'

I waited nervously, but after several minutes, true to her word, she rang back with the information.

'I can book a flight to Amsterdam plus Rome for a small extra charge. QANTAS and British Airways are fully booked, but I think I can book you with another company that does have one late cancellation in tourist class.'

I would have preferred Business class of course, but perhaps I would be an anonymous traveller in a crowd of tourists.

'That's fine,' I said, much relieved. 'Do you want my credit card number?' I gave her the details quickly.

'Thank you.' She added that the ticket would be waiting at the airport desk. 'Your friend can pick it up there if that's alright, Mr Harrison?'

Her innocent question threw me off balance for a moment, but I managed to say, 'Yes, thank you, a very close friend. What time is the flight, Rachel?'

'Midday, don't forget your friend is to be there an hour before take-off,' she reminded me.

I had no intention of being exactly on time, of course. The latest I could get there without actually missing the flight was my aim, to give my pursuers little chance of joining the flight. I carefully replaced the bug by the same method. I then rang Peter on his mobile and invited him to a game of squash at midday at the squash club on the Eastern Shore.

He was understandably puzzled and not keen at first, but I managed to persuade him and he sensed that it was important that we meet. A rough plan had formed in my mind as to how to escape my observers, because I was now sure that I was being closely watched, as well as being bugged. If I was getting a bit twitchy, it was understandable after Loader's near demise.

To complete the illusion, I changed into squash clothes and put my normal clothes in the backpack. I then put the squash racquet into the bag, with the handle prominently showing in case I was being watched.

After nervously double-checking the contents of the bag again, I casually walked out to the carport and, in full view, placed the bag carefully on top of the Jaguar XK 140 Sports. The car had been sitting unused for several days, so it would be good to give it a hard run. I took the bag off the top of the car and nonchalantly put it on the front passenger seat, praying that the car would start, which it did at the second attempt. I let it idle for a few moments to warm up to working temperature and to give the impression that I was in no particular hurry.

Peter and I had bought the 1960 3.8 Litre XK Fixed Head Coupé together as an investment, but so far had only managed to have the engine and mechanicals fully restored. The body was to be worked on next year and maybe the year after that could be an official entry in the following year of the Targa Tasmania event. Kate was not concerned, but called it overgrown schoolboys' dreams. Maybe she was right.

My idea was to leave the farm and drive towards Hobart and the Eastern Shore where the squash courts were, then drive past the airport entrance road at speed, and turn off at the roundabout junction to the small township of Cambridge. I would then reverse direction quickly and zoom back to the airport. If I was being followed, I would then be going in the opposite direction to my pursuers.

The engine was running beautifully as I manoeuvred steadily through the town and onto the next town of Sorell. The traffic lights were red so I came to a smooth stop and looked in the mirrors – so far no sighting of my expected hunters. I relaxed a little when the lights changed to green and the Jaguar moved calmly off.

As I turned the wheel, I glimpsed something briefly in the mirror that I didn't want to see – the dark blue limousine turning out of the pub car park opposite. I accelerated quickly. The engine, now warmed up, raced away and was soon travelling well over the speed limit. I was moving far too fast as I reached the edge of town. The big limo behind me had obviously shot through against a red light. Now I knew my plan to drive into Cambridge had to work or I was sunk.

Managing to put a few cars in between us was my aim, and I quickly accomplished it, although dangerously. The causeway between Sorell and Midway Point was only a two-lane highway, with holiday traffic in both directions, so the limo had little chance of closing the gap. The water on either side glistened and sparkled in several shades of blue. It was quite distracting and I checked myself for letting my attention wander as I nearly clipped a red Mini coming the other way.

The roundabout at Midway Point was coming up fast. I sensed that, with luck or skill, I could put some further distance between us. The Jaguar's tyres squealed in protest as I tugged hard on the steering wheel.

The next causeway was too close, but I managed to pass another campervan dawdling along, stickers blocking out some of the rear window, I flashed my headlights as I passed.

There was still no chance for my pursuer to gain on me, the traffic was still heavy and seemed to be creeping along. The road was still too narrow for either of us to overtake and so the status quo remained. More frustrating for him, I reasoned.

As we came through the lightly wooded area with the golf course on one side, I realised I had to make a quick decision. Should I turn now into the airport road with five or six cars between us, or go straight on to the service station, where I planned to turn around and double back?

I chose the latter. The airport roundabout proved no problem for the Jaguar and I took it fast. Now I had an almost open road; a couple of light trucks were loafing along, the drivers oblivious to anyone else. Hoping that they wouldn't change lanes, I passed them at almost twice the speed limit. I slowed slightly, checking the mirrors. The junction was coming up soon, much too soon in fact, because I was going so fast I almost missed it, the loose gravel on the side road making a harsh rumbling noise. The limousine was not gaining at all and he negotiated the right hand turn untidily.

The road curved slightly to the left, and so I was able to conceal the car by driving into the service station and parking on the left side behind the fuel pumps. As I screeched to a halt, the young attendant rushed out of the office with a big welcoming smile on his face when he saw me. His face changed to astonishment as the limousine swept past at speed, accelerating hard, the engine straining as he stood on the throttle. There was no sound of screeching brakes as it roared off round the next bend.

He was now on the old airport road, which was very pretty, but quite twisty and undulating, and he would be struggling at that speed to keep the big car on the road. It would be several minutes before the driver realised he had been tricked and either turned around in the narrow road, or roared on toward Hobart.

What I had noticed with dismay, as the limousine raced by, was that there were only two occupants, which probably meant that the third man was kicking his heels at the airport waiting for me. I smiled and waved to the young attendant who now had a totally mystified look on his face.

I turned the Jaguar around the triangle of grass in front of the service station and drove off again in the opposite direction, back to the airport at a more sedate pace. Much to my satisfaction also, the local police passed me in the opposite direction, chasing after the limousine and showing no interest in my car at all. I also noticed, with fiendish gratification, that two or three marker poles on the roadside had been smashed, obviously by the big limousine. The rental company wouldn't be too happy about that.

Driving into the airport car park, I waited at the barrier gate for my ticket and then put it in the glove box. Peter had his own keys and so I parked the car as near as possible to the main entrance. I grabbed my bag from the front seat and strode quickly up to the service desk. As I collected my ticket, the pretty young brunette looked somewhat taken aback by my scruffy appearance, with ruffled hair, perspiring heavily and still dressed in sports clothes. I was the last one on and a few holidaymakers ahead of me gave a few curious glances. The airport security also removed my squash racquet, which was old anyway.

So far so good, but where was the airport watcher, the third lookout man? Surely he must be around here somewhere. Was he still in the car park, in the terminal, or possibly in the queue ahead of me?

Discounting the latter possibility, I boarded the plane, found my seat and stowed the backpack in the overhead locker. My seat was at the rear of the plane near the toilets. Fortunately, it was a window seat because, as we taxied out to take off, I could just see, but sadly could not hear, the limousine with two swarthy men gesticulating furiously and about to start a fight. One of them, clearly the senior of the two, was pointing at the plane and obviously shouting at the other. The situation was about to reach a crescendo when the familiar sight of the police car arrived and calmed them down.

A policeman's life is not a happy one, I surmised. I realised they were not the same two policemen who came to the farm the previous evening. The two swarthy characters would probably come up with some plausible story about missing a friend on the plane, but would have trouble trying to explain the high-speed chase and shooting through a red light at Sorell.

chapter 3

The Journey Begins

The plane took off smoothly. I looked down and could see the sunlight glistening on the clear blue waters of Frederick Henry Bay. The cabin crew went through their usual routine safety procedures and the elegant woman next to me commented that they must get bored doing that every time. I politely agreed with her and from that moment she and her fourteen-year-old daughter entertained me on the one-hour flight to Melbourne. They were going on a shopping spree and then on to the cinema later.

During a break in the conversation, I slipped into the toilet as discreetly as possible and changed into holiday clothes and lightweight walking shoes. If I had to move quickly in the airport at Melbourne, then I must maintain my anonymity and be able to slip through the busy throng. As the plane continued on, I tried to think what had occurred yesterday.

Firstly Loader: why had he chosen me? Was he really impressed with my skill and knowledge as a calligrapher, or was it flattery? He seemed sincere, although with Loader you could never be certain. He was as cunning and devious as befits a man in his position. He didn't reach that point without being shrewd and able to persuade people to do things that they sometimes didn't want to.

Why, I also wondered, was he so openly casual about bringing the information to me? It was careless, I thought, and most unlike him. Why didn't my pursuers tackle me in the middle of the night; and where was the third man?

Then I remembered the old photograph. I hadn't got it. The last time I remembered seeing it, Loader put it carefully back into his overcoat pocket. They would have checked over his belongings before finally throwing him in the cattle pen, so now I must believe they had a clear idea of what they were looking for. They also had my book, *The History of Writing*.

I realised that Peter and Kathy could also be in danger and the boys too, and I felt very responsible. I was determined to ring Peter as soon as possible, immediately when I reached Melbourne.

My troubled thoughts were interrupted by the excited young girl sitting next to me, wanting to see the view of the city as we flew in and landed in the airport.

I had less than an hour before I had to board the flight to Sydney. As soon as I could, I found a phone in the terminal and rang Peter on his mobile number. Peter was angry and somewhat mystified by my irresponsible actions and couldn't understand what I was trying to tell him.

'Are you in trouble?' he said. 'Is it money they are after? Because two Italian-looking blokes in a limo turned up at your ruddy farm when I went to look for you? They questioned me aggressively about your leaving so abruptly and I said I was as nonplussed as they were.'

'That's a good answer,' I replied. 'I can't tell you the whole story, it's far too complex. But no, it's not money.' I thought very carefully about what I should say to get Peter and Kate out of the limelight. 'Peter, you must tell the local police about the visit and tell them your concerns. These people have tried to catch me already and failed and they are very upset.' Upset was a totally inadequate word for it, they must be spitting chips, I reflected.

'Jack,' he paused, 'for heaven's sake be bloody careful. And come back in one piece.'

'Will do. Regards to Kate and the boys. Must go, don't want to miss my flight. Oh, Peter – there's a man called Loader in the Royal Hobart Hospital, he will tell you all you need to know.' Loader would tell Peter enough to satisfy his curiosity and no more.

As I turned to leave the phone, I was aware of someone standing very close behind me. He was swarthy, solidly built, with black shiny hair and a day's growth of stubble on his chin. Making my way quickly to the gate indicated on the information screen, I wondered whether my telephone conversation had been overheard; and if so, why? Was it necessary for him to stand so close? Was he someone I should be wary of, or was he in a hurry to use the phone? I twisted round to try and catch a glimpse of him.

He was talking animatedly into the phone. Well that's what telephones are for, I mused. Was I getting too apprehensive? I tried to put it down to tiredness and nothing else, and yet – where was the third man; the loose cannon rolling around the deck? He had a distinct advantage over me, almost certainly knowing what I looked like, but I had no idea what he looked like.

I just caught my connecting flight to Sydney and found my seat with the help of the flight attendant. As I sat down, my unshaven friend appeared in view and found his seat about five rows ahead of mine. I consoled myself with the thought that if he had any evil intentions he couldn't do anything now. Tiredness was going to be my biggest problem, so I dozed fitfully until the snacks and drinks were served.

The food was refreshing and helped settle me down and I nodded off again, only to be woken up by the general hubbub of the people around me as we approached Sydney's Kingsford Smith Airport.

Sydney and Melbourne are both cities of approximately four million people now, and the mock rivalry between the two is legend. Melbourne inhabitants in the 1890s seemed to think it was the Paris of the Southern Hemisphere, such was the pride in their city. It is the birthplace of Australian Rules Football and the Melbourne Cricket Ground was where the 1956 Olympics were held. Sydney, on the other hand, is justifiably proud of the Harbour Bridge, the Opera House and of course, being the host of the 2000 Olympics.

But for all that, I preferred Hobart and the relaxed lifestyle and pure air of Tasmania. You can keep the world's big cities. It was only twenty minutes drive from Hobart city centre to my hobby farm in beautiful unspoilt countryside.

As we trooped off the plane in Sydney, each passenger making their way to separate destinations, I tried to see what my unshaven friend would do. I followed him for a while and then he made his way to the toilet. That was my chance to put on some speed and I increased my pace, checking the information board again.

The transit lounge was beginning to fill and so I picked a position where I could see most of the comings and goings of passengers. Someone had left a newspaper lying on the seat next to mine so I started reading it, with occasional glances to see if anything untoward happened; but nothing did. At least, not to worry about.

I breathed a sigh of relief as we finally boarded. I was obviously overtired and anxious and, before I dozed off again, the sight of Botany Bay, the birthplace of Australia, reminded me of a calligraphy friend who had flown over to Hobart several times and given me encouragement in my early struggles with calligraphy.

I wanted to sleep through most of the flight to Singapore – only the chink of glasses and the smell of food kept waking me. I managed to stay awake long enough to finish my food.

Suddenly the plane lurched violently and then sank. One of the overhead lockers fell open and spilled its contents partially into the passageway and hit a flight attendant. The oxygen masks came down and the seatbelt sign went on. The plane repeated this uncomfortable bucking around manoeuvre several times, but finally it seemed to even itself out.

The calming voice of the Captain came over the intercom, explaining that we had run into some clear air turbulence due to updraughts and that we might be delayed at Singapore while the plane was thoroughly checked for damage. The injured attendant was helped by her colleagues to the back of the plane and, from the conversation I overheard, it appeared she had a broken collarbone.

Clear air turbulence is something that happens as a result of updraughts from mountains and can't be seen by radar or visually, therefore it's most unexpected and can do damage because of its unknown nature. We were just unlucky. It was necessary for the airline to stop and check for damage at Singapore, but from my point of view, it was a delay I didn't want.

Once again we were all huddled into a transit lounge to await results and I quickly tried to pick a seat where I might be unseen, but could keep a watch for my unshaven friend. He came in looking rather tired and with a worried look, sat down some distance away from me – and surprisingly – with his back towards me. He seemed to be entirely alone and didn't speak to anyone.

I still wasn't sure if he was the third man or not. As I glanced occasionally in his direction, he appeared to go to sleep. Then the seat next to him was vacated and another tall swarthy man came and sat next to him and started talking to him in a rather conspiratorial manner. I took an interest in this manoeuvre because, every so often, they would look around the transit lounge as if looking for someone. I guessed they were talking about me but, apart from visiting the toilets, there was nowhere to hide. He got up reluctantly and made his way in my general direction. Then he saw me and veered straight toward me. This was the moment I had been waiting for; it might clarify what was going on.

He stood hesitantly in front of me then he said, 'Excuse me, can I speak to you?'

'I suppose so,' I said. 'Under the circumstances I have little choice. What do you want?'

'Well, that fellow over there wants a private conversation with you. I don't know what about, he wouldn't say, but he tried to slip me fifty dollars to persuade me to talk to you, pointing in this general direction as he spoke.'

I studied his face carefully, looking for some reaction. 'What's your name, where do you come from, and what's your business in all this?' I said swiftly.

He looked directly at me. 'My name is George Simeone from Hobart. I'm an electrical engineer, my wife's just about to give birth, and my mother is seriously ill in hospital in London. And I don't know anything about this "business" as you call it.'

The answers came so swiftly and without hesitation, and he hardly took breath until he had finished. I felt that perhaps after all he wasn't involved and was telling the truth.

'Well, George Simeone, you're getting into something unpleasant and my advice is to keep out and stay out.' He was standing close enough to me to cover my actions. I pulled out my wallet and slipped him a fifty dollar note. 'Now, tell him I'm coming over and give him his money back and say that you want nothing to do with this, you understand. You're Italian aren't you?'

'Yes, sort of,' he replied. 'My mother is English but my father is Italian. Hence my surname and I don't want your money either.'

I smiled at him, 'Why did he ask you to be a messenger?'

'Because he saw us together at the telephone I suppose, and thought I knew you.'

I could discern an element of truth in what he was saying because I also noticed a slight cockney accent. 'Okay, George, now go, and don't look back.'

I counted thirty seconds and then stood up, putting my bag on my shoulder and ambled over to the figure he had indicated. He was wearing an expensive, well-cut suit, Italian style – and that's about the only pleasant thing about him. His eyes were shifty and his face was pock-marked. He seemed unlikely to be a hit man or a heavy weight boxer, bit on the slim side for that, I reasoned. As I approached him he flashed an uncertain smile, showing a gold tooth in the front.

'Thank you for coming,' he smiled again. 'Could we discuss a little matter, which we both have an interest in?'

'Oh? What's that?' I said with a straight face.

'Come now, Mr Harrison! We both know what that is.'

This time he didn't smile and I sensed a touch of evil in his voice. He must be the third man from the limousine and he also knew my real name. So much for the replacement passport Loader had supplied me with, I thought. I was beginning to feel rather vulnerable, because it hadn't worked.

'Let me put it to you simply,' he continued. 'My employer wishes to buy what you are searching for and is prepared to offer a large sum of money.'

'Who is your employer?' I asked casually, turning away from him to survey the lounge to see if he had any back-up tough guy. He appeared to be alone. He didn't answer.

'I'm not interested. Sorry to disappoint you,' I said harshly, and began to walk away. He started after me and caught my arm. I looked at his hand and then looked straight at his unpleasant face. 'You had better not do that again,' I said sternly.

'Harrison, this is a good offer we are making you. Don't forget that. I will ask you again later.'

I disliked the way he said my name – it grated on my nerves. 'You are an ugly piece of work and I don't like your face.'

I spun him round so that his back was hard against the column. 'And in future,' I continued, 'don't involve innocent civilians in your dirty little schemes – understand?'

His face became red and his eyes told me his anger was about to explode, but before he did anything, I stood back slightly and patted him on the upper arm in a pseudo-friendly fashion, as if we were old friends from way back. I spun round on my heels and walked away casually.

Round one to me, I thought. But it probably wouldn't be so easy next time. I didn't look back, but I sensed the emotion emanating from behind me. Neither did I look for the electrical engineer. He must be left out of this at all costs. I returned to my original seat and waited to re-board.

Eventually we boarded the plane to Amsterdam, which is the longest leg of the trip. I knew from previous trips that flying can be very tiring, apart from the body clock being thrown into total confusion.

Before going to sleep, I went through the events of the last two days again, because some things were not as they should be. In spite of that I slept soundly, or at least as well as one can in the tourist class.

My thoughts were still inconclusive and I must have slept through one meal because, when I eventually woke, I was hungry, still feeling like a zombie, and my mouth felt terrible.

To get my blood circulating again and stretch my legs, I went for a walk up and down the aisles, at the same time checking to see if the smart-suited Italian from the Singapore transit lounge was in the tourist section. No sign of him, so I assumed he was in Business Class. I rather cheekily poked my head into the Business Class while the attendants weren't looking, and I could just see the top of his head. One of the stewards eventually noticed me and questioned me in English and French, but I shook my head, smiled and pretended not to understand, backed out, and regained my seat. Business Class passengers are conducted from the plane before Tourist Class, so he would probably be waiting outside in the airport terminal at Amsterdam.

If I were going to slip past him I would have to be one of the first of my group to leave, this was my immediate first thought. That would be very difficult, as my seat position was right in the middle, so some other scheme would have to work. If I could delay as long as possible my departure from the plane when we landed, perhaps he would imagine I had sneaked past him. I realised that would be my only chance, or I was in trouble again.

Time to re-assess my position – I compared my advantages to my disadvantages. First: I knew where I was going – eventually, but they didn't. Second: although they had the old sepia photograph, only I knew where it had been found and that I would have to go back to the middle of Wiltshire at the end and start the real quest from there when I reached southern England.

Did the Italian group, who I assumed were the Mafia, have a link with the IRA? I doubted that very much. The IRA might want to present the pages to the Irish Government themselves, or even some extreme faction of the organisation might want to destroy them entirely. God forbid. On the other hand, the Mafia would hardly want it themselves, but would sell it to some immensely rich collector for drug money. The chances that they would work together also seemed decidedly remote.

Finally we arrived at Schipol Airport, Amsterdam and, following my plan, I hung back as long as possible in my seat until it went silent and I was certain the plane was empty. As I was about to move a stewardess came along for a final check and spotted me. I explained to her that I had mislaid my passport.

'Surely not,' she said. 'You must have had it to get on the plane.'

I smiled back, 'Would you help me for a minute? It must be around here somewhere.'

We searched together and suddenly she said, 'Found it!' with a look of triumph on her face.

I had purposely placed it a row or two in front of my seat. 'It must have slid forward when we landed,' I said.

I seemed to be forming a sympathetic relationship with her so I boldly said, 'I wonder if you could help me with some advice? I need a small, quiet hotel as I have no booking and I don't know Amsterdam at all.'

'That's no problem at all,' she replied swiftly. 'Although it's not approved of by the company, you can come in our taxi into the City. I will show you a most reasonable hotel. It's small but very nice.' I smiled and thanked her.

So I travelled into the city with three charming young women, who were very happy now that their tour of duty had finished. They dropped me off and I paid the fare to thank them. I was so weary I didn't notice the name of the hotel. Finally I got to my room and fell into a deep sleep almost instantly.

The next morning I awoke and looked at my watch. I had slept for over ten hours and I felt much revived, although with a slight headache. I reckoned I had some time to spend, as the plane to Rome was not until mid afternoon. A brisk walk in the fresh air would benefit me and I desperately needed breakfast. Because it was a little late, my stomach was sending me frantic messages.

The hotel had no lift, so I skipped down the stairs only to find I was too late for breakfast. The kitchen staff were preparing for an early lunch. Walking a short distance, I managed to find a cosy restaurant that looked as if they served everything on the menu at any time. The waiter spoke passable English and so I had an excellent cooked English breakfast, followed by a large cup of tea. I paid the bill and strolled out into the spring sunshine. I had no map of the city, but I didn't intend going very far anyway.

The city was in the early stages of spring, and I found it enchanting with the flowers and early buds on the trees starting to sprout. The place seemed alive and busy and, just for a short while, I felt in a holiday mood. Canals were everywhere and the streets basically follow them – and one canal with charming old buildings looks much the same as another if you are not concentrating on where you are wandering. I took a few photos, checked them for quality, and then glanced at my watch. I realised time was moving on and I should return to my hotel to check out and get my passport.

I became conscious of the fact that I hadn't the faintest idea where I was, not a clue. That didn't worry me at first, because I could buy a map and follow that. That might help, but I was also aware that I didn't know the name of the hotel or its street name. Simple enough to solve, I thought – all I had to do was retrace my steps. That was not easy, but after about half an hour of seemingly going round in circles, I found my way back to the cosy restaurant where I had such a pleasant breakfast.

The waiter who had served me smiled, waved and called me over as he cleared away the dishes from a table at the front of the café. 'There is a friend to speak with you,' he said. I looked around puzzled. Where I thought! He couldn't know that I knew no-one in Amsterdam. At that moment a dark-suited figure I instantly recognised moved out of the dark shadows from inside the restaurant.

'Ah, Harrison, there you are. We meet again.' His voice had a smarmy sound of triumph. 'You had us worried. We thought you might get lost, so I had Lucero Visentini follow you. You don't mind do you?'

I was aware of movement behind me, and as I turned round, a hand landed on my left shoulder. It was the hand of a large man. Visentini was huge and he was grinning as I completed my turning movement. There was no escape.

'Yes, I do mind,' I said quickly. 'It's "Mr Harrison" to you.' Visentini behind me clamped my shoulder tightly and I felt a slight nudge in the back, which could be a gun but could also be his index finger. Surely he wouldn't be so stupid as to have a gun in a public place in broad daylight, but I couldn't afford the risk of moving quickly.

'Meeting you again has not been a pleasure and you are spoiling a beautiful day,' I continued calmly.

'So sorry, Mr Harrison, but the day isn't over yet. Please remember our consortium is offering you an enormous amount of money.' He lowered his voice towards the end.

I managed a cynical laugh. 'Which is it to be? An "enormous amount of money" or a "large sum", which I think is what you offered me before. And now you are a consortium. Would you ask your large unpleasant friend to take his hand away from me?' I said fiercely.

He looked at Visentini and made a slight movement with his hand. The vice-like grip on my shoulder relaxed. 'I cannot give you exact figures of course, it is not my position to do so,' he said.

'I thought not,' I replied sarcastically. 'What is your position, apart from annoying me and slowing me down?'

'You have important business and we are trying to help you. We have men everywhere. You cannot escape from our surveillance. Why don't we sit down and talk over a cup of coffee?'

'Thank you, no coffee. I have a plane to catch to London. I'm on holiday and I don't want to see either of you again.'

'Mr Harrison, be reasonable. You cannot do this on your own. We can help you,' he continued, with an almost polite tone in his voice.

I sensed he was beginning to think that it was better to butter me up than to get in my way. After all, we were both searching for the same thing, although obviously not for the same reasons, of course. He attempted a smile which was not convincing.

It wasn't true that I was going to London, but it might confuse them a little if I told them that, and then made my way to Rome. It was worth a try and it might work. These people were dangerous, but also cunning, and they knew their nasty business. If I was to outwit them, I had to be equally cunning.

'I'll make a deal with you,' I said, trying not to sound sarcastic. 'When I find anything I'll let you know.

'You can depend on it,' he said drily. 'We will be on your shoulder all the way.' He had a slight smile of triumph on his face, as if he had gained the upper hand.

Not if I could help it I thought. 'We must now end this conversation, but I must congratulate you on your command of the English language,' I said with a straight face.

'Thank you,' he said. 'I learned much when I worked in a night club in London.'

I said a silent 'thank you' for that information. I decided to push my luck a bit further. 'If you are going to be on my shoulder, as you put it, perhaps you should tell me your name.'

'Ricardo Mazuchelli, but good friends call me Ric,' he said proudly. 'A fine Italian name, don't you think?' He was still trying to convince me that he was friendly.

'I'm sure it is. Tell me, does Visentini speak English?'

'No, he does not. He speaks very little, enough to order a meal only!'

'Well then – to show your good faith – can you ask him to come round to the front of me where I can see him? I don't like him hovering around behind me.'

He spoke in Italian to Visentini, who moved very reluctantly around me. I understood what Mazuchelli had said, but I didn't disclose the fact. 'That's better. Now we can all see one another. You must excuse me – I have a flight to catch,' I concluded.

'Don't forget, Mr Harrison, our offer still stands,' he said, in a conciliatory tone.

I made my way quickly to the hotel and collected my backpack, checking that everything was still there – which it was – but the few contents had been rearranged slightly. Obviously my gear had been searched very carefully, but not, I was certain, by the hotel staff. Whoever had searched was disappointed to find no clues. Indeed, there were no clues, except for the information in my head and Loader's envelope, which I kept with me at all times. If Visentini had followed me around Amsterdam, it must have been Mazuchelli who persuaded a hotel staff member to let him search my room. He had wasted his money.

I gave the hotel manager a surly look as he returned my passport. I thought briefly about asking him whether he had any nosey visitors while I was out playing the tourist, but I didn't have time. I knew something had happened because he seemed unable to look me straight in the eye, or smile. I settled the account without the usual thanks or a smile.

ROME

T he coach to the airport was smooth and quick, and I was on the flight to Rome almost before my mind had cleared its mixed emotions. The beguiling charms of Amsterdam had relaxed my senses, and Visentini had followed me quite easily without my noticing.

Loader wouldn't be pleased with my slack behaviour: Too much the tourist and not enough concentrating on the difficult task he had set me. I made a mental note to concentrate, sharpen my reflexes and not make any more mistakes. My physical condition was excellent, probably better than it had ever been, but I had lost some of that sharp edge in the finer points of hit and vanish – so essential to staying alive in this strange business.

Fortunately, Mazuchelli had thought carefully and considered it essential to keep on my tail and only observe. Although, when the time came, he would have no hesitation in killing me. The right time for him would be when I had the missing pages in my hand.

I dozed fitfully on the plane, except for the magic moment when the plane was just flying over the Alps. It was one moment of fog and cloud, the next moment bright blue sky and sunshine below as we started flying over northern Italy.

When I awoke from dozing yet again, I realised the plane was preparing to land at Fuimincino Airport, Rome. We were right on schedule and I would have to extract myself quickly from the airport. Although I had made an effort to slip out of Amsterdam, there was no sure way of knowing whether I was now free of surveillance. So far they had obviously kept a close watch on me, and twice had found me when I thought I was free. I didn't trust them, and what was more troublesome was that they seemed to have enormous reserves of manpower. It was, perhaps, a measure of the importance they placed on this project.

I didn't want another slip-up and Loader's voice kept interrupting my thoughts. I paused for a moment and realised his opinions and values were not mine, and so I decided to trust my own judgement.

I was more concerned about getting it right for myself this time. Loader wasn't here, so I had to make all my own decisions. This quest was even more interesting than I first realised and I was keen to bring it to a successful conclusion. I remembered my father mentioning that one of our ancestors in a previous century was an antiquarian. I casually wondered if genetics had anything to do with my interests. A more genteel subject in those days, I realised, but far more cut-throat now in the 21stcentury.

However my first task, as soon as I had settled into the hotel that Loader had chosen in Rome, was to research all the information I could from the Vatican Library. I took Loader's notes and checked his details, addresses and the name of a hotel.

His advice seemed to be to go straight to the Vatican Library and he enclosed a letter of introduction to a Father Kelly.

He will give you all the help and information you might need. He speaks several languages including of course Latin, but also French, Italian, Greek, Middle English and of course Modern English. Father Kelly is a great linguist and scholar.

I read the name and address of the hotel a couple of times so I could give it to the taxi-driver without halting when I needed to direct him. I wanted to sound confident as if I knew the city really well.

As I made my way toward the exit a smartly dressed young man detached himself from a group of taxi-drivers and strolled toward me. He had been deep in conversation with them and had turned round when one of them had said something to him. It was possible he was waiting for me, or someone like me, but I couldn't be sure. But it might have been prearranged by someone. I realised I must still careful and be on my guard.

He sauntered up to me and smiled, '*Buon Giorno, Signore.* Can I be of help? Do you need transport in to Rome? I have a fine modern taxi waiting.'

I waited for him to continue, but he didn't say any more and just stood still, eyeing me up and down. This slightly unnerved me, because I wasn't expecting anyone to meet me. I looked at him carefully to see if he was carrying any armament. He didn't seem to be armed – no tell-tale bulge in the jacket. I noticed him gesticulating more with his right hand, so the armour, if any, would be on his left side.

'OK, you'll do! I want a smooth ride into the city and I would like to see some of the sights of Rome.'

'You won't regret it, Signore. I know all the best sights. I also can find you a fine lady, if you wish!' This clumsy remark seemed so unnecessary and convinced me he wasn't part of any prearranged welcome plan.

'Just the sights, thank you. I'll leave the other part alone.'

The young taxi-driver was enjoying himself in the usual Rome Grand Prix. It was almost afternoon rush hour and he was driving very close to the small Fiat in front; so close that, if any driver up ahead made the slightest error, we would be in the biggest mess imaginable. I purposely insisted that I sat in the back behind the driver, so that by leaning forward imperceptibly I could watch in the mirror any car following us. I noticed only one that stayed at a discreet distance behind us all the way into Rome. Although it might be pure coincidence, I decided it was better to keep a close eye on the situation anyway.

'Can you drive around the Roman Forum and the Colosseum – slowly please? I want to see it properly.' I took a few photographs just in case, for the record.

He nodded without saying a word. He slowed slightly and eased into another traffic lane.

I noted the street names to reassure myself. We swept around the end of the Colosseum and, as we turned, I checked the mirror again. It was a white Mercedes following us, but it had dropped back slightly.

'Okay. Can you go right round and park nearby – over there, now?' I indicated quickly.

He shook his head, 'No, not possible there. I get into trouble – tourist bus stop.'

'All right, I understand. Drive very slowly then.'

He complied, being very careful, while I pretended to admire the magnificent ancient structure, also keeping a watch occasionally for the white Mercedes by checking in the mirror. The other car kept well back, but was still lurking behind us. I still wasn't convinced one way or the other as it pulled in several places behind us.

'Right, take me to the hotel now.' I almost shouted the order at him and he took off at a fast pace. I had chosen my moment carefully, because a tourist coach came round the corner slowly with a line of traffic behind it. That should keep the Mercedes blocked in for a while as the coach disgorged its passengers.

'What hotel, Signore? You didn't say.' I glimpsed a look of puzzlement on his face as he skilfully navigated his way into the stream of traffic.

'Hotel Internationale. Just go to the Piazza Colonna, it's near there.'

'As you say, Signore. I go fast now, I know it well. It's very new.'

We pulled up at the hotel. It was an impressive new building obviously meant to cater for international tourists. I paid him quickly and watched him briefly as he roared off. He turned round the Piazza and made his way in the general direction of the airport. As I reached the entrance the commissionaire strode confidently toward me with one hand holding the door open, while the other saluted me. Not my kind of hotel – too much gloss and glitter. And I felt totally out of place with my backpack.

Approaching the booking counter, it was obvious they were accommodating an important medical conference of some sort. I decided to get out if I could, although Loader had booked the hotel room, he hadn't given me an exact date. If my room was not available, that was fine with me.

In the spacious entrance hall was a large marble fountain quietly playing in the middle. The flags of all the nations represented were hung from the mezzanine floor with a prominent sign welcoming all the international medical delegates. This was why Loader had given me a new passport in the name of Davies. The desk clerk obviously had a difficult day, but still managed a polite smile as I gave him my name 'Richard Anthony Davies', and also my false passport.

He checked it and left it on the counter as he ran his finger up and down the lists on several pages, stopping every so often and muttering to himself. He stopped on the last page. 'Here we are Dr Davies, sorry to keep you. You are in Room 528, near to Dr Thompson. He is also from London in Room 529.'

I asked him what time the restaurant opened and he replied that because of the conference they were open nearly all the time; in fact they were opening again in a few minutes.

'Good, I understand it is an excellent restaurant,' I said. He assured me proudly it was the finest and newest in Rome.

As another guest arrived, I swiftly took my passport back and held onto it waiting to see if he noticed and moved quickly towards the elevator while he directed his attention to the next arrivals. As I turned, the smart lift attendant in a new uniform held out his hand for my scruffy backpack, which seemed so totally out of place in this palatial hotel. I politely declined his offer, but he insisted on accompanying me to the elevator and he pressed the button for my floor.

As we stood together waiting for the doors to open, I glanced out through the main entrance to see the white Mercedes draw up outside and two men get out obviously in a great hurry, because they didn't bother closing their doors and rushed through the foyer past the startled doorman.

So far my luck had held, but this seemed like a big problem. The doors opened just in time and I stepped inside the elevator and pressed the button for the fifth floor. My pursuers were almost at the doors when I shoved the young man out of the lift and straight into their path. Anger and frustration were written on their flushed faces as the doors closed. I was tempted to say something, but I ignored them deliberately.

The elevator rose smoothly and quickly to the fifth floor, but before getting out I pressed the button for the top floor in the hope that it might confuse my pursuers. The doors closed and I waited briefly to make sure the elevator was on its way up to the top and then pressed the call button. Precise timing was essential as I ran down the corridor and found Dr Thompson in room 529. I furiously banged on the door. Nothing happened, so for good measure, I repeated my action on several other doors as I made my way to the fire exit.

Then everything happened at the same time: the elevator doors opened, also several people came out of their rooms, just as I opened the fire escape door. I had hoped to cause as much chaos as possible, but as I opened the fire escape door to the staircase, it set off the fire alarm which was a bonus.

By the time I had reached the grand entrance hall, total confusion reigned, which was perfect for my purpose. It was obvious that the fire alarm had not been used before and the hotel staff had no idea what to do, or how to direct the international visitors. There was much talking, shouting and waving of hands, but no clear directions to the guests. I slipped unobtrusively across to the restaurant and found my way through the splendid kitchens, which were now empty.

The kitchen staff were standing around outside, chatting and having a quick crafty smoke, and took little notice of me. I nodded and smiled at one or two of them, but didn't make any eye contact. My plan seemed to have worked, so I walked in the direction of the Vatican City, hoping to find a small inconspicuous family hotel.

The taxi had dropped me off near the Piazza Colonna which was just beside the Via Del Corso. Coming out of the rear of the hotel led me in the general direction of a large triangular area between the Corso Vittorio Emanuele II and the Tiber River. This was so much nearer to the Vatican City and an easy walk for me in the morning. After half an hour's meandering around the myriad of small streets, I soon found exactly what I wanted – a small hotel. I hoped it was inexpensive, because also this was not what my pursuers would be expecting.

chapter 5

change of plan

The hotel was precisely what I was hoping to find tucked away in a narrow street, friendly and much nearer to the Vatican City. Loader's idea had merit, I will admit, getting me lost in a conference of doctors who were perfect strangers. Who would think of looking for me there? My new abode, however, was only half an hour's walk to my destination, as I soon found out. Here I was in Rome at someone else's expense and enjoying work that I had always wanted to be closely involved with.

The following morning I felt so much better and strode out past the Ponte San Angelo, and briefly glimpsing the Castel San Angelo, I made my way to the special entrance as instructed on Loader's detailed sketch plan. After nervously knocking on the door it was answered by a young priest who spoke English well enough for me to explain my mission. He led me through long corridors with marble floors. The quietness had a feeling of tranquillity and peace. Finally he stopped at a door and knocked, a kindly voice answered and we went in.

Father Kelly, a sprightly man of nearly sixty with grizzled hair, rose from behind an enormous carved desk and came toward me, his hands outstretched in greeting. 'Ah! You must be the young man Mr Loader wrote to me about'.

I was unsure about his accent but it sounded slightly Irish American, perhaps even Boston. I gave him the letter of introduction which he swiftly read. 'Ah! That's excellent', he exclaimed and smiled. 'Shall we start immediately? I have several meetings this afternoon, but this morning is completely free for you.'

I felt a sense of relief that he was so welcoming. 'Tell me, have you seen the *Book of Kells*?' he said, beginning the conversation. Regretfully, I had to tell him that I had not – yet.

'Ah, you must indeed see it. Every time I manage to go to Dublin, I make a point of seeing it. I believe Edward Johnston, your famous great English calligrapher, regarded the *Book of Kells* and the *Book of Durrow* as the greatest glories of calligraphy'.

He then went on to say that he was delighted to help me in any way he could, but expressed some reservations about finding anything about the *Book of Kells*. He showed me many manuscripts from various centuries, countries and different styles, some in Greek and some in Latin.

'Now come with me and I will show you your special room that we have set aside for you'.

I followed him down another long corridor and went into a room which although compact, had everything a serious researcher needed: a desk with good light, a light table for viewing slides, and a computer. He handed me an ornate key and as he did so asked me to keep the door locked even when I was working, and especially if I left the room. He showed me so much and it was a massive learning experience that I had not expected, as he explained how everything worked. Then he excused himself and left me on my own.

I was so absorbed in the information that he presented that I forgot about lunch and it wasn't until hunger pains made me glance at my watch that I realised the time: it was nearly two o'clock. There was a knock at the door and Father Kelly let himself in with his key and tapped me on the shoulder.

'Tomorrow is also a day, you know my friend. You can continue your research then,' he said with a smile. 'You must come again.' I promised that I would return, because although I was feeling exhausted, hungry, and my mind was going into overload, I was extremely happy with my research so far.

'It is gratifying to have such an interested student,' he said. I nodded and smiled. I was in my element if the truth was told. 'I am very pleased and feel honoured to be here thank you. Tomorrow I will return,' I replied.

The next day he spent even more time with me, recounting the incredible history of the fifth and sixth century Christian Church in northern Europe that was largely centred in such places as Jarrow and the Isle of Lindisfarne off the North East coast of England, and the Isle of Iona on the North West coast of Scotland. Iona, because of its remoteness and safety from the Vikings, also perhaps contributed to its original Celtic style. The scribes and artist monks drew on several monasteries in Switzerland and Italy as well as the Coptic influence from Egypt, and possibly Syria.

The trade from the Mediterranean along the coasts of Spain and Gaul had continued for centuries before and Ireland had benefited greatly from this inter-twining of knowledge. Finally, in about the seventh or eighth century, calligraphy flourished into a religious art that culminated in he *Book of Kells* and the *Lindisfarne Gospels* although the *Book of Durrow* was earlier from the last part of the seventh century.

This great art form came to a sudden and vicious halt because of the Vikings, who pillaged and plundered the monasteries. The raids began in 793AD and destroyed the Monastery of Lindisfarne on the North East coast of England. Fortunately, the monks managed to hide these great Gospel books in safe storage, and because they were written on vellum, they are almost as perfect as the day they were completed and are still to be seen and marvelled at in the 21st century.

Loader was correct in stating that Father Kelly was a learned scholar and linguist, but what he didn't tell me, or perhaps he didn't know, was that he was also a knowledgeable calligrapher, so we compared notes and paid particular attention to Irish Half Uncial and the *Book of Kells*. I was in great awe of him.

At last he said, 'I have composed a small booklet that might be of help to you. It is the fascinating story – part of which I have just told you – from my long research I have studied over the years. This is the result of my labours,' he said with a smile. 'But will you promise me one thing – if you find those missing pages, please let me know?'

'I promise,' I replied, 'and I will also go to Dublin and the library of Trinity College and your book will be my *vade mecum* – as my aid.' We shook hands, parted with a smile and the young priest conducted me to the door.

The third day was fine and warm and I was eager to start my quest at the library. Picking up my backpack, I made sure I had Father Kelly's booklet and my notes and set off for a small café that specialised in early breakfasts. The waiter took my order and while I waited, I took out Father Kelly's booklet and re-read certain passages that were of particular interest. It wasn't really a booklet, but was more comprehensive, containing many footnotes which caught my interest. The waiter returned with my order and I paid him and continued reading.

While sipping the coffee I heard a familiar voice and a light but distinctive laugh which I could not mistake. A party of tourists were passing by and in the rear of the crowd, obviously having joined them for cover, was Jacqueline, who was hanging onto the arm of a good looking young man with dark hair. They were – or seemed to be – playing the part of newly-weds, judging by their giggling behaviour, but as they passed me they stopped laughing and then walked on.

Jacqueline held her hands behind her back with a pink handkerchief and two fingers of her right hand pointed downwards. This could mean only one thing. I assumed it was a signal to me to join them in the second café on the right. I pretended to take no notice and carried on at the same pace, drinking coffee and finishing my breakfast.

Casually rising as if nothing had transpired, I continued strolling and found them as I expected in the second café on the right. Jacqueline had been the one special woman in my life for a while in London during my time with the Department, but because of the obscure and difficult nature of my work, and never knowing where I would be, the whole affair fizzled out in a blazing argument, which was painful for both of us. Now here we were sitting opposite one another in a small café in Rome. Jacqueline was hanging onto the young man like a new bride and behaving unnecessarily over the top.

I frowned at her and said, 'Can you tone it down a bit, it's embarrassing?' Her face changed immediately, 'I was asked to play a part and I'm doing my best,' she said crossly.

'Who asked you to play a part?' I questioned her gently.

'Who do you think? Your awful boss – Loader,' she said in a whisper.

'For Pete's sake Jacqueline, there aren't any secret microphones in here. Start at the beginning and bring me up to date. I'm surmising there is a change of plan – why?'

'Sorry, Jack, I am forgetting my manners. Let me introduce my new husband. This is David Guthrie.'

She winked slightly as she spoke and laughed and showed me her wedding ring and engagement ring. My mouth dropped, because it was the engagement ring I had given her. She hadn't returned it and I hadn't asked for it back. Some things are best left unsaid. She read my thoughts.

'Well, I didn't have time to get another one. Anyway, it's David's job to bring you up to date with the latest information.'

'Okay,' I said, 'your turn David, it's all yours.'

He leaned across the table. 'Firstly, although you are getting on well, I assume, Loader wants more action and he is upset that you changed your hotel because he wants us – me, to keep an eye on you. We cannot protect you, if you don't stay in the right hotel. He believed it was a good cover. I disagreed with him but kept quiet.'

I raised my eyebrows and said, 'I don't need protection, thank you! Tell me, who was it that followed me from the airport? Was that you in the white Mercedes?'

He raised his hands in a questioning manner. 'No, it wasn't us, we were following them in our dark green Jaguar. Much less obvious, don't you think?'

'Agreed, but you weren't where you should have been, which is why I changed my hotel. Loader's not always right you know. What the hell was he thinking?'

'He is my chief in this affair – I just follow instructions,' he said rather angrily.

'I prefer to think for myself, so you can tell that to Loader. I like to do things my own way. Tell him I'll return to London tomorrow.' I was lying of course, but I didn't care. 'David, would you do something for me?'

'Yes, sure,' he replied casually.

'Pay a visit to the toilet,' I said in a slightly arrogant tone, 'I have a few words to say to my ex-fiancée. Don't rush yourself.'

He left us and was obviously not pleased to be spoken to in that way. Jacqueline was not happy either and chided me. 'That was a bit unnecessary of you. Are you alright?'

'Sure I am, but why did you become involved in this? I mean you knew vaguely what I did for a living and couldn't cope with it. Now here you are'.

'Loader promised me it would be simple. No problems, and a few days in the Eternal City with an allowance in cash and all fares and hotel paid for. Besides, I was wondering about you.' She smiled and looked me straight in the eye as if to say, I'm over you but still curious. I thought how stunningly beautiful she was, bright, intelligent and with a delightful sense of humour. How could it have all gone so wrong?

'You're looking very well and still gorgeous, you know,' I told her with sincerity.

'Thank you. You're looking fit and well too. Must be your new life in Australia'. I raised my hand slightly from the table and said, 'Tasmania, actually,' and chuckled.

'By the way,' she said, 'I've just finished illustrating a new book that's coming out in September or October for the Christmas season. Keep your eyes open for it in the bookshops. They paid me plenty – *un sacco di soldi* as they would say in Italy.' I remembered that she was well schooled in the Italian language.

'We just say "a truck load" in Tasmania. Same thing I guess. But I must get on now.' I leaned across the table and put my hands gently around her face and kissed her on the lips. I slowly got up from the table. 'How is the old bastard anyway,' I asked.

'Out of hospital, limping slightly and with his jaw wired up,' was the quiet reply.

'Promise me you will pass the message on to Loader,' I said.

With one last smile and a wave I left and went to see Father Kelly, but not by my usual route which had obviously been discovered, but by a more complex route.

Now my plans must change. After all my fascination and interest in the Vatican Apostolic Library, which contained one of the world's most magnificent depositories, I felt disappointed, but now I knew clearly what was I had to do.

I arrived at my usual door and knocked loudly. The young priest opened the door and he seemed surprised to see me. 'You're late today sir, please come in,' he said quietly.

I was in two minds about whether to give my message directly to him and ask him to pass it on, but thought it would be most impolite not to give a full explanation to Father Kelly after his great interest and help.

I followed the young priest down the long corridors again and he showed me into the room. Father Kelly rose and he could see by my face that something was wrong.

'Father, I'm afraid there has been a change of plan. Loader has asked me to return to London soon. I must thank you for all your attention and kindness, but I will keep both my promises.'

'Well, my young friend, life is full of disappointments. But you must remember that the Lord moves in mysterious ways, his wonders to perform.' He came forward and took my hands together. 'It's been such a pleasure to help you in this quest. I will pray especially for your success in the forthcoming days.'

I thanked him and then asked if there was another door that I could use to leave the Vatican. He was momentarily puzzled, but then realised why. He obviously understood, and nodded. He gave direction in Italian to the young priest who then took me to a different door, shook hands and let me out.

Returning to my hotel quickly, and ensuring no one was following, I entered the small foyer and met the head of the family hotel. I explained my reluctant decision to leave, paid my bill, and asked him if he could arrange for a tourist coach to pick me up to go to Florence and then on to Venice. He raised his eyebrows in surprise.

'You have missed the early morning coach, but I will try for the 11 o'clock coach.' He made a quick phone call, and with a look of triumph, carefully wrote down the details. He drew a route on a small map of Rome, in red pen, and called a taxi for me.

The taxi ride once again was fast and furious and we reached the Piazza dei Cinquecento just in time. Before I could get my breath back, we were away through the streets of Rome.

The coach was almost full and seemed to consist mainly of Americans, Australians, New Zealanders and a few Britons. I settled down to chat with the British couple on the opposite side of the aisle, about how things were in Britain. Eventually I dozed off; the journey to Florence would be about three hours. I estimated we would arrive in enough time to be in our hotel before the evening meal.

I had been hoping to pay a quick visit to the Biblioteca Laurenziana in Florence, which could also contain many valuable documents of interest to add to my knowledge. The Biblioteca was originally designed by Michelangelo to contain the books of the famous Medici family. I realised that I would be unable to visit this time, but perhaps would do so in the future.

The coach made a scheduled stop at a large complex of shops, car park and restaurants along the Autostrada. Everyone climbed out of the coach and wandered into the shop to buy a few items or a meal. I purchased something for my camera and a snack, placed them in my pack, and we all wandered back to coach.

But for me it was not to be so simple. Putting my foot on the first step and looking up at the coach driver who was speaking to a police inspector, I distinctly heard the word *Inglese* and *criminale* – which was a worry.

There was a sudden movement from behind me and I was being hauled away from the coach by two burly heavy-handed policemen, who had quietly crept up without my noticing them. I had little or no chance to protest, because they applied an arm lock on me and frog-marched me to the waiting police car.

As soon as we were clear of the complex, they stopped again and wrenched my bag from my shoulder. They went through it thoroughly, taking out everything and placing it on the ground by the side of the car: maps, camera, clothes, passport and Father Kelly's book. They showed great interest in the book, but didn't make much sense of it because it was written in Latin, Greek and English.

They looked at my false passport and compared it with me, asking several questions about my medical degree. Seeing that my profession was meant to be an ear, nose and throat specialist, I had a difficult job of convincing them and ended up almost miming and drawing diagrams, but surprisingly the senior officer seemed happy with my fake explanation.

Suddenly his attitude changed. He looked rather disappointed and apologised in English, with some difficulty, that there had been a gross error and it had been a case of mistaken identity. I was slightly suspicious of his explanation.

'And, now we go catch your coach – very quick,' he said. I quickly repacked my bag and we drove off at high speed, sirens sounding and lights flashing. At the high speed we were travelling, we should be catching up with the coach very soon. Suddenly, I sensed that this was a ruse.

Looking more closely at their uniforms, I noticed that they were not brand new – they were a bit shiny and the badges were rather dull, and then the driver started smoking a pungent cigarette. This signalled to me that they were definitely not the genuine article, but there was little I could do, with the driver in the front and the other two on either side of me on the back seat. It was a tight fit, so I said nothing and didn't make a move.

Eventually the sign for Florence came up but we didn't stop, taking a wide sweep around the south and west of the city. There was no explanation from any of them as we sped along, so I kept quiet and just observed. The driver, who was obviously the leader, then lit up another cigarette, at which point I leant forward to object by tapping him on the shoulder. I received a massive punch to the side of my face which rendered me senseless.

Still feeling groggy, the next thing I remember was the magnificent St Mark's Square in Venice. I was being pushed through the narrow streets and piazzas. The crack on the jaw could not have caused this sudden loss of my faculties. I was jammed in a rather old wheelchair, unable to move my hands or legs, but I could observe where I was. They must have drugged me for safety while I was unconscious, but with what? Trying to move my limbs, I could feel that I was strapped up with packing tape and covered with a blanket to make me look like an invalid.

Receiving a few sympathetic glances, we made our way across St Mark's Square in front of the magnificent Cathedral. Feeling totally out of control, I simply looked and nodded back, smiling.

The thug who had viciously attacked me, muttered grimly in my ear that if I spoke out I would get more of the same treatment. It was perhaps better to remain silent and bide my time, gather my strength and try to clear my head, which was still hurting and buzzing ominously.

We slowly trundled our way through the fascinating streets of Venice till we came to a charming but small palazzo. The door was opened and despite my condition, I was immediately entranced with a wonderfully decorated and well kept flagstone courtyard, set with brilliant coloured flowers and a small fountain in one corner. Someone had an eye for beauty and design, but not this bunch of thugs; they were only the heavy brigade doing the upper controllers' bidding – I wondered who that someone was; who really owned the place.

They roughly pulled me out of the wheelchair and undid the lower bindings, so that walking was just possible, or at least with very limited movement.

With great difficulty and a few painful kicks, I managed to climb the stairs, and we went through several immaculately decorated rooms. Some one was obviously proud of this rented Venetian gem. Finally we arrived in a room which had African spears and shields displayed alongside 15th century oil portraits on the walls of this elegant villa, which seemed very strange in a small Italian palazzo. Obviously, the rich owners had travelled the world and collected many items of interest on their travels. The room was immaculately furnished. There was plenty of food, fruit and drink in expensive bowls and dishes laid out for a meal.

Unfortunately, this was not for me I realised, because they now roughly pushed me through the room and down a long, badly lit corridor which led to what can only be described as a general purpose room lined with shelves. I noticed a few small garden tools, hammers, screwdrivers and boxes of oddments. It had an old wooden chair, which they unceremoniously dumped me on. When I tried to protest, one of them smashed my head back against the metal column behind me, and proceeded to tape my head to the column and re-taped my feet at the ankles.

The whole operation was painful, but they enjoyed every minute, and laughed at my intense discomfort. Having satisfied themselves that I could not escape, they left me in solitary isolation and I started to breathe more easily and considered my very uncomfortable position, which at first assessment didn't look at all favourable.

They left the light on in my makeshift prison, the switch being outside the door. When they locked the door, I listened for the noise of the key being removed, but they left it in the lock. But of course it was on the outside. There was a small window with bars on the outside so that was no help either, but as I sat there grimly cursing, I saw a small possible line of hope. The door, which opened inwards, had two hinges and one of them was not properly fitted; the pin in the top hinge was partly in the up position. It had been fitted very hurriedly.

Heavy footsteps were coming down the corridor. The door rattled and opened, and the third man, much younger than the other two, entered carrying a paper cup with hot minestrone soup in it. He then proceeded to undo the tape around my mouth and helped me drink.

'No more – gone,' he said and then taped my mouth back to the column behind me. Our eyes met briefly and I tried to thank him, but couldn't. I think he understood. Then he went out and locked the door. I listened again for the key to be removed, but it wasn't. I realised this could be helpful in planning my escape.

Loud music started drifting down the corridor, as well as shouting, singing and laughing. They were obviously celebrating their successful day. Meanwhile, the packing tape was proving very awkward to remove from my hands, but after two hours of desperate twisting, flexing and turning my bonds, I was free. The rest of the tape was comparatively easy to remove, but my wrists were red and inflamed because my blood flow had been restricted.

The noise from down the corridor gradually subsided and then finally fell silent. Listening for any footsteps, I quickly searched around the room for some sort of small screwdriver to push the hinge pin further up and out at the top, but it proved difficult to move.

Looking round the room, I found a small can of oil and a hammer. Plying the hinge with oil, I tapped the screwdriver upwards once, as gently as possible with the hammer, and listened for any reaction from outside. There was no movement, so I tapped again and listened. No sound! The pin started to move at last. There was a noise from down the corridor so I stood still for a few moments, not moving and hardly breathing.

Silence returned, so I continued very gently and extracted the pin. Trying the other hinge-pin was more awkward, because it was the lower one and difficult to get down to, but finally it moved, slowly but surely. I replaced the top pin just enough to hold the door in position. because it might fall into the room with a tremendous crash.

The effort of all this was very energy sapping, so I sat down on the old chair again to regain my strength and get the circulation back into my arms and legs. I was very tired, hungry and wanted revenge, having been beaten and humiliated. My face was still hurting, particularly my jaw. They hadn't loosened any teeth, but it wasn't from a lack of trying. In spite of all the damage they had inflicted on me, there was nothing that wouldn't heal eventually.

I checked the time on my watch, it was four a.m. There was still no light from the sky, only from the gracious villas and palazzos opposite. Feeling sore and stiff, I heaved myself up and put my new plan into action. Putting a wad of cardboard under the door on the side of the lock, and using the brass hook on the back of the door, I removed the top hinge pin and slowly brought the door inwards.

I stepped into the corridor. There was no reaction from the end room, except heavy snoring from at least two sleepers. I replaced the door by putting the hinges back together, left the light on and locked the door from the outside. I hoped to fool them by leaving the key in the door as if I was still in my prison.

Feeling my way silently along the corridor in the darkness was easy until I almost reached the door at the far end. It slowly opened and a very sleepy and very drunk, bulky figure came out. It was the bruiser who had belted my jaw in the car. We both reacted with shock, he thinking he had seen an apparition as I materialised out of the gloom, but I recovered first and a solid blow to the solar plexus stopped him moving.

As he sank to his knees, I hit him again fiercely in the face and there was the crack of a breaking nose. Before he fell and made any noise, I grabbed him by his hair and shoulder and dragged him head first along the corridor to the room which had been my prison.

He was out cold. I turned him over and trussed him up like a chicken. Tying his left hand to his right leg, and his right hand to his left leg, I then bound his mouth tightly to prevent him from screaming a warning. My revenge was almost complete, but there were two more thugs to deal with and I realised I had no plan except to play it by ear.

Finding my bag untouched in the room was easy, and I scooped up a supply of bananas, apples and bread, putting them in my coat pocket.

There was a faint noise of somebody moving or turning over in their sleep. I stood still and looked around. There in the corner was the youngest of the three, the one who had given me the cupful of soup. He had just woken up and in the semi-darkness had not realised immediately who I was. He regained enough strength and tried to leap to his feet in panic, then partially collapsed to the floor.

In that moment of almost comedy, I tried to wrench a spear from the wall, but for obvious reasons it was well held and it took another violent pull to release it. I damaged the plaster on the wall, leaving a large hole. He however, had partially recovered and was about to launch himself towards me. I brought the tip of the spear round and pointed it at his throat. We were at a stalemate, but with the odds decidedly in my favour. I asked him his name and he answered, 'Lorenzo.'

'Where is Capitano – Il Capo,' I shouted to him, as I twisted the point of the spear aggressively nearer his throat. Seeing that he didn't have the upper hand, he just shrugged his shoulders in a resigned gesture. 'Gone away Mestre . . . Prostituta.'

'Okay, where is your gun,' I growled. He didn't understand. 'Where is your *arma automatica, pronto*?' I held out my left hand.

He understood that and he moved slowly over to a chair, unsteadily, because the tip of the spear was very close to his throat all the time. He groped in the side pocket and pretended to look for it, but I realised it was in the holster of his leather belt which was somewhere hidden in the room.

I threatened him again with the spear and said '*Errore grande*' – he understood my bad Italian accent and reluctantly produced the leather belt from underneath the table.

'*Al rallentatore,*' I said and motioned to him to put it on the table slowly. He did so reluctantly, but by now he was too scared to do anything rash. I had no intention of killing him, but I could not relent in my aggressive manner.

I motioned him to move away from the table, switched on the light, took the gun out of the holster, and checked it. It was not standard issue for Italian police, which did not surprise me. It was a gun that I didn't recognise – it had Russian markings on it and a calibre that I could only guess at.

There was another gun to be accounted for, that was owned by the bastard who had tied me up and put me in the general purpose room. I walked around the table and while I held the gun looked for the third holster. It too was on the floor and I indicated to Lorenzo to place it on the table slowly; which he did. This one turned out to be a 9mm Beretta pistol. It was heavily scratched and looked fairly old, and was loaded. It had a seven-round magazine and had probably been stolen at the end of the Second World War. I felt more at ease with this one, having used it in training in London.

Although my situation was improving, I now perceived two problems, one was Lorenzo, who looked more like an impoverished art student than a Mafia thug. He was about 20 years old and seemed out of place in this business. There was no one at this time of the morning to ask how to get to the airport and I needed to neutralise Lorenzo. Deciding to use him to direct me, I ordered him to get dressed in ordinary clothes and said, '*Aeroporto presto*,' and he quickly caught on to the idea.

He seemed reluctant, but finally agreed and we left the villa silently. We made our way through the deserted narrow alleyways, he in front with me closely behind, with an occasional push or prod from me to let him know I meant business.

Realising that I couldn't go into the airport with the gun, I took it out of my pocket and unloaded the damn thing when he could not see me. At every opportunity I dropped the 9mm rounds into rubbish bins along the way. He almost spotted me as he turned anxiously round – I gave him a swift push and he kept going. I kept one last round in the gun for my protection.

We saw only two or three people and the occasional collection of scrawny cats as we passed the still water of the minor canals and a few lonely bobbing gondolas. Eventually, we reached the Grand Canal which was starting to gather a few early workmen – I assumed they were there to collect garbage. It was now six in the morning and the early light was quite bright, but gave very little warmth. The Vaporetti water bus was waiting and I made Lorenzo pay the fare and stood close behind him.

The water bus took us to another stop where we walked over a series of pedestrian bridges to where a normal taxi would take me to the coach terminal for the airport. This I thought was now the time to part, but things didn't work out as I expected. Coming toward us was the leader of the three and he quickly got off the bus; he was one of the first to disembark, aggressively shoving his way through the holiday makers. I gave a sharp jab to Lorenzo's kidneys and muttered, '*Silenzio!*' viciously in his ear.

He didn't move as we waited till the other man disappeared into the crowd on his way back to the Palazzo. He will get a disagreeable shock when he arrives at the villa and I couldn't resist a smile of triumph.

Making sure the leader had gone, I ordered the younger man to stay on the dock here and said, '*Restare qui* – Stay here,' pointing down emphatically.

He replied, '*Si* – okay'. I moved the Beretta in my jacket pocket, but he sensed I wouldn't use it in a public place except in a dire emergency. I watched the water taxi turn and steadily make its way back to Venice and then I joined the crowd getting on to the bus for the Marco Polo Airport.

My problem was still the wretched gun, so I started eating the fruit out of my pocket and before I had finished I put the gun in the folds of the banana peel and put them in a rubbish bin on the way to the airport entrance. Making my way to the shops in the main concourse, I bought a replacement jacket of a mid-grey in the lower part and charcoal in the upper part with a high collar and a hood. This was a very Italian style, I believed, and would be entirely different to my old jacket, which I casually left in the gent's toilet after swapping everything over.

Then I checked the contents of my backpack and it was starting to smell rather unhealthy. It seemed sensible to change that too, because my appearance would then be entirely different. So I chose a new backpack which had the Italian flag on it. Strolling over to the British Airways counter, I found that the tourist class seats were taken. I was glad to be able to take a seat in business class because I felt I needed a bit of comfort after the troublesome events of the past two days.

ChAPTER 6

ESCAPE FROM VENICE

As we came into London Heathrow I caught a glimpse of the city which I hadn't seen for a couple of years and my spirits lifted for the first time since I left Hobart. It was a comfortable flight and I felt refreshed and had dined properly for the first time since leaving Rome. My confidence returned as I believed I had given my pursuers the slip, or so I thought.

I took a taxi and told the driver what sort of hotel I needed and he complied, assuring me that he knew the perfect place. It transpired that he and his brother had a major interest in a modest private hotel situated in a peaceful square in South London.

The hotel had been skilfully renovated, a grand Edwardian house, solidly built and immaculate. Harry the taxi driver insisted on carrying my bag although there was no need. His brother Dennis, the hotel manager, was very friendly and asked me where I was from.

'Tasmania,' I replied. He looked up from the hotel register and said 'Oh! I know, the island below Australia,' he said, with a smile of triumph.

'Yes, the Island State of Australia,' I replied.

Dennis informed me that afternoon tea was now available. It sounded good to me and was to be followed by an evening meal which was satisfying, but without any alcohol, because I still had the headache that I had received in Venice. I requested some headache tablets which helped tremendously. A good night's rest in a comfortable bed was just what I needed.

My bag had been taken to my room, so I removed my shaving bag and put it in the modern en-suite bathroom which was cleverly designed with a short narrow vertical window on one side. Feeling much safer and comfortable, I retired to bed early and slept soundly.

I contemplated my next step. My prospects were looking brighter, but the thought that nagged my mind was that every turn or move of position that I made seemed to be countered by my pursuers. To achieve this cat and mouse game indicated an enormous amount of manpower and of course money. They were like evil shadows around me. The quest was indeed now very serious, more that I realised when I agreed to take it on. Loader knew it was important, but even he didn't know or realise how dangerous it would turn out to be.

Early the following morning as I was finishing shaving in the en-suite bathroom, I was mulling over some of the strange things that had happened.

How, for instance, had they been able to keep track of my route in spite of the last minute changes I made? Was it something they had known before or had someone, including Loader, leaked some information back at the farm in Tasmania? Perhaps they had got something from the literary Professor when he lost his life tragically in the bizarre car crash on his way back to Oxford. Was it possible they were responsible for his death? Most likely it would seem so, but there was no clear answer.

So I let the matter rest and I decided to go to Wiltshire immediately and bypass the Bodleian Library at Oxford for now. This was a pity, but it would save time and I now felt more confident of my calligraphy, or at least the history, because of my visit to the Vatican Library with Father Kelly and the booklet he had given me.

Just as I was finishing packing there was a furious knocking on the door and before I could answer, the door burst open and a young lady, looking very flushed with a concerned look on her face said quickly, 'You'd better get downstairs – Dad's blazing angry because there were two men here saying they were from the Accommodation Bureau or something, demanding to see our guest list. Dad didn't believe them or me either. He told them to shove off in no uncertain terms or he'd call the police! That worried them and they muttered something in a foreign language, which we didn't understand.'

'Probably Italian, could it be?' I said. She nodded. 'Could be, it certainly wasn't French,' she replied. 'I speak French very well at school, second in my class,' she said proudly.

She went over to the en-suite bathroom and slowly opened the small narrow window a fraction, enough for me to see out. There was no surprise for me; it was as I expected. I glimpsed the man I had head-butted in Venice, now wearing a plaster on his nose. Revenge would be uppermost in his mind. 'Do you know those men?' she whispered.

I grabbed my bag and followed her downstairs to the foyer to be greeted by Denis with a thunderous look on his face; not at all pleased by the events of the last few minutes. I was unable to placate him with a brief outline of my quest. He was still not impressed, and brushed my explanation aside.

'I need to get to Oxford as quickly as possible,' I said, shouting back in a similar manner. 'I have no car, but they do, and it's imperative I arrive there before them.'

He looked at me gravely with hesitation and disbelief, as if he was unsure of my story. However I gave him my credit card to pay the bill, he studied it, turning it over rather suspiciously and then shrugged his shoulders resignedly as if to say, 'I have no choice.'

At this moment, his brother Harry burst in through the front door, with a puzzled look on his face and then looked at us all in turn, waiting for an explanation. I started to speak but Dennis rudely butted in. 'He needs a ruddy car to get to Oxford today – you brought him here – you sort it out!'

He turned his back on us and strode angrily towards his large desk. They were behaving like a pair of ex-boxers, although Harry seemed to be the calmer of the two and grasped the tense situation. He took the phone and tapped out a number. He spoke calmly and clearly, so we could all hear and understand him, giving his instructions to the female voice at the other end of the line.

Finally he turned to me and said he had fixed it, meaning the car hire. He gave me his business card and said, 'Show this to Theresa, that's my missus. She will know what to do, give her your credit card. Now go out the back door, through the kitchen garden, turn right and along the lane to the street until you come to the service station and car hire office.'

He then turned around to Dennis who had calmed down somewhat and said, 'You're coming with me in my taxi to draw them off. We will make for the centre of London somewhere – at high speed. 'You two ladies', indicating the mother and daughter, 'lock the front door after us – alright?' They nodded in agreement. 'And don't open it till we get back in about half an hour.'

There was no time to shake hands, or thank them. I followed his plan and ran quickly along the lane, which in gracious Edwardian times would have been the servants' entrance, and reached the service station and car hire office. Theresa was swift, and understood what was needed. The car was nothing expensive, but a popular modern Ford that would fit in with the day-to-day traffic I was about to encounter.

I was on my way as soon as I saw Harry's Taxi move off loudly accelerating through the gears, and followed quickly by the other car chasing after it.

Creeping out tentatively at first, I drove sedately in the opposite direction, in other words, in a westerly direction. Although my knowledge of London was reasonable, it was not perfect, and I was now searching for a sign which said Bath and Bristol. Having found the M4 I then changed direction to the M3 in an attempt to confuse any possible pursuers and ended up near Gatwick Airport, Manning's Heath and Horsham.

It was then I realised I was being followed by a black Mercedes Benz. My confidence did not expire, but I was now certain I was again being followed very skilfully. I drove onto the by-pass, which circled Horsham, at a leisurely pace to pretend I was not in any hurry.

The Mercedes was still following, and there was no way I could out-pace the more powerful car, so I carried on round a series of roundabouts and finally came up behind the Mercedes hopefully confusing them entirely and lastly turning off quickly onto a minor road. The sign said Winchester, the Cathedral City which was the old capital of the Saxon and Norman Kings of England. The reason for my twisting and turning through Southern England was to throw them off the scent. I was frustrated because it hadn't worked the last time and it hadn't taken them long to find me.

Another plan was now essential, because they now knew the number plate of my car, so I circled around Winchester. I then found the A30 to Salisbury, which was a fairly straight road. Reaching the old city of Salisbury safely, I hoped to exchange cars with an old college friend named Dick Cooper, who ran a specialist car tuning business. His multiple skills included rebuilding classic and modern iconic 'Automobiles of Distinction', as he put it on his brochures. It was the ideal time to put our long friendship to the test. I hoped that this new plan would work.

His complex had grown considerably since my last visit, so business was obviously booming. As I drove into the customers' parking bay, my friend Dick Cooper approached me and a look of recognition and total surprise came over his face and he grinned as I got out of the car. 'Jack, I thought we'd seen the last of you when you went to Van Diemen's Land.'

I smiled back warmly and said, 'It's now known as Australia, you ignoramus, or to be exact Tasmania in my case.'

He invited me into his office which was impressive. The walls were now covered with large photographs of the many cars he had restored, tuned, raced or had some hand in improving. They were a fine record of his achievements.

'Quite a show,' I nodded, 'congratulations on your success.' I said pointing at the display on the walls.

We talked on about other subjects such as university and marriage, and he then surprised me by saying he was married with one boy and they were expecting another baby this year. Of course that led him to ask me about my old girlfriend Jacqueline, and so I told him of my bad luck in the marital stakes and an abridged version of why I was here and what my quest was about now.

Academically we were very different, but got on very well and the one thing we always had in common was an interest in cars. He went into automotive engineering and made, I now believe, a wise move.

I then felt it was time to explain what I needed and why. He shook his head. 'It's almost impossible,' he said. He paused and thought again. 'Well, there is one possibility, we use it as a mobile test bed. It's licensed, insured and ready to drive and works well. It's an old Austin 1800 with a bored-out engine, balanced and tuned to perfection, but the bodywork is very rough looking. I can show it to you to see if it'll suit your needs and then we can go for a drink at the local pub.'

St. John's Alley, Devizes.

It sounded good, although I was slightly disappointed about the bodywork. But beggars can't be choosers, I thought. The car, however, turned out to be a great surprise. Admittedly the bodywork was rough as he had described it, but when he opened up the engine bay it was a joy to see. The engine was immaculate with twin carburettors. Dick went on to explain what else he had done to the engine, polishing the head, lightening the flywheel and then triumphantly finished by telling me it would do over 110mph. In that way it was perfect for my purpose, because although it didn't look like a fast car, it would be fast enough for me.

'You will look after it, won't you?' he said with a smile. I nodded in agreement, although I didn't fully realise what I was promising. We went off for a drink and carried on reminiscing about our past adventures.

The arrangement was to swap cars and then be on our way. The pub was warm, friendly and inviting, so he suggested I stay the night there. It was a most attractive idea but the day was moving on and I felt that I should go to Devizes to continue my search. We parted reluctantly as we swapped cars. The old Austin 1800 seemed to love the straight roads; it certainly had a plenty of zip about it.

I drove along past Old Sarum, which was the original medieval hilltop city of Salisbury, passing the mysterious Stonehenge, which is older than the Pyramids and up on to Salisbury Plain itself, and on through the various villages on either side of the road. Some areas were classified as 'DANGEROUS,' I noticed, and only for the use of the British Army for military manoeuvres. This word struck me as odd, as manoeuvres could mean 'possibly deceptive.' I grinned to myself as I found most military matters frequently deceptive.

I reached Devizes well before sunset, the engine not missing a beat. I started looking for antique shops as I drove down Long Street, past the Town Hall and into the rather pleasant Market Place with its many fine Georgian and Victorian buildings. I drove around the town looking for any potential places to stay the night, but came back to the Market Place. The old Bear Hotel looked charming and worthy of my custom.

I booked a room immediately, went into the bar, bought a beer and got talking to the barman. Although at first he seemed unlikely to know a lot of local history, he surprised me with his extensive knowledge of the town and its splendid historic buildings. I questioned him about shops and in particular antique shops. It seemed very promising with regard to the latter.

My sole reason for choosing Devizes was because it was in the centre of Wiltshire and there had been a settlement there since the Bronze Age and if I drew a blank I could use it as a base for further searches. Although Swindon in the North was bigger, it was comparatively modern, having expanded rapidly from a village in the 19th century when the Great Western Railway developed. My instructions from Loader were not exact; possibly because of the minimal information from the literary Professor from Oxford, as a result of his sudden death. My complex search would have been so much simpler if I had not had to follow Loader's instruction to go to Italy first. The only benefit of my trip was that I had broadened my knowledge of historic manuscripts and my time in Rome had been an added bonus.

The Bear Hotel was about four centuries old and was an important part of the town, apparently a Borough since 1141AD. When I had driven into the town earlier, I had noticed the Museum of the Wiltshire Archaeological Society. It seemed a good point of enquiry, and also an antique shop close by.

I gathered much information from the barman, who was also a car enthusiast and knew of my friend Dick Cooper from Salisbury. He wished me luck and finished his shift for the night, then handed over the bar to a colleague, who also gave me more information. In the entrance foyer was a stand full of pamphlets and brochures extolling the virtues of Devizes and the surrounding district with maps of the town. I chose the most promising ones after enjoying my meal.

So far my search had been a bag of mixed fortunes, leaving a trail of mistakes from Tasmania to Devizes, but I was learning quickly. Taking the pamphlets to bed and glancing through them for knowledge of the area, I found one of them contained a good local map. I finally turned off the light and slept soundly, eager for the next day.

SOME SECRETS DISCOVERED

E arly the following morning the view from my bedroom window was a scene of bustle and lively activity, the whole place was preparing for the weekly market. Dressing quickly, I decided to cross over the road and went into the cake and coffee shop directly opposite the hotel and climbed upstairs to have breakfast and carefully observe the Market Place activity below.

The car which I had so casually parked outside the Bear Hotel seemed to be under close observation by a tall figure. Looking through my camera at maximum long focus, I could see who it was; he was still wearing a plaster on his nose but a smaller one than before. He was obviously waiting to interrogate me.

I finished my coffee and cake, paid and casually went downstairs. I waited for a large group of young people to come strolling by and I joined them, keeping in the middle of the group and kept walking towards the Brewery at the far end of the Market Place.

As soon as I deemed it safe to move, I crossed the road and strolled back towards the hotel, keeping well in and slipped down Station Road by the side of the Corn Exchange. I entered the old hotel by the original rear entrance and ran into the first barman, the car enthusiast, now sporting a tee-shirt with several motoring badges and logos. Greeting him like an old friend, I invited him to drive the Austin around the town to see what he thought of it. He was nonplussed at first, but readily agreed when I explained that my friend Dick in Salisbury had worked on it.

He took the keys and gave me a quizzical look, and then he was eagerly away to test it out driving around the town. My idea was to hopefully lead my shadows away for a while so I could seek out any antique shops in the town.

I waited until the Austin moved off and then there was furious movement outside. Another car started up, there was a slamming of doors and a roar from outside the hotel, then an eerie silence as peace returned. My first step out of the hotel confirmed that my watchers had followed him.

Walking swiftly, but without bringing attention to myself, I went back the way I had driven into the town towards the Museum, arriving at the antique dealers I had noted yesterday and went in.

'Good morning sir, can I help you?' asked the distinguished elderly gentleman. 'Is there anything in particular you are looking for?' He smiled in a pleasant way and looked every inch an expert.

'Yes, there is actually. I'm looking for old photographs pre-Second World War if you have them.' I was approaching the subject carefully on purpose, because I didn't know what might have happened before my arrival.

'Well,' he paused and thought before answering, 'we have many old photos of the Devizes Castle and some of the local villages. There are some at the back of the shop and we have portraits of local families, and identities that show the old style costumes back in the Victorian era. I also have some really old Daguerreotypes. But that is not quite what you want is it? They are very old, as you probably know. And valuable to a specialist collector.'

'They sound interesting. Perhaps I could have a look at them all,' I replied casually. 'Are you a photographer, or a collector? Or both?' he queried. I replied that I was a bit of both, which seemed to satisfy his curiosity.

He took me into the back room where he had more photographs. I thanked him and sat down with two rather large trays of photos that he offered me, unsorted. I chose a Daguerreotype which he said was in excellent condition and well preserved, but he told me to keep it closed and out of the light. He then mentioned that another gentleman some weeks ago had shown interest in some of the photographs.

'He had also shown great interest in photographs particularly of calligraphy, but never came back again. He seemed to be one of those professor types, you know. I put them away somewhere safe and now I can't remember where they are. My business partner might have sold them without mentioning anything to me.'

My spirits rose rapidly and then fell immediately. 'How long ago was that?' I said. 'Oh, let me think, it was about three . . . or maybe four months ago,' he replied.

It sounded ominous, but promising. At that moment another customer came in so he left me on my own at the back of the shop for a few minutes. There was a brief conversation but I couldn't hear what was being said.

He came back quickly and said, 'Incredible! Absolutely incredible, I can't believe it. He was looking for old photographs too. I showed him what I had in the front of the shop, but he didn't show much interest. Didn't look much like a collector one little bit.'

He watched as I studied the photos. I went carefully through them, there were so many. Then he got up and said as he walked to a filing cabinet, 'I should have the Professor's card in here. Now let's see if I can find it.'

I carried on with my search as he let out an exclamation of triumph. 'Found it, I knew I would find it. It's all coming back to me now.'

He handed me a business card which I studied carefully, so now I knew who the mysterious searcher was – Professor George Grant. I was now on the right track at last.

'Thank you very much,' I said. 'Do you know why the Professor didn't come back?' I couldn't tell him the real reason and that I knew the answer already.

'No', he said, 'it was rather strange, because he seemed so fascinated and excited, but he didn't explain why'.

Time was flying by and I was worried about the old Austin. 'Are there other antique dealers in the town?' I said.

'No, however there is a second-hand dealer in Monday Market Street, although they are unlikely to have anything like this that you are looking for. I tell you what I'll do – I'll have a thorough search and also ask my business partner. He is much younger than I with a better memory. Why don't you come back at 5.30 just before we close? Hopefully we'll have something for you.'

It was a good idea, so I paid for the Daguerreotype, which he carefully wrapped. I estimated he was in his mid-seventies and perhaps should have retired, but having such a love and vast knowledge of his antique business he didn't want to.

I shouldn't have worried about the old Austin, because as I crossed the road it zoomed past me. As I reached the safety of the other side, he came alongside and shouted something at me and carried on to the Bear Hotel. The second-hand dealer was an interesting experience, but did not produce any useful results, so I walked around the town until it was time to eat and stopped at another pub in the hope of absorbing more of the local knowledge, or any other useful information that mattered.

I was keeping out of view and so at the end of the afternoon I strolled back to the antique shop only to be greeted by the worrying sight of an ambulance and a police car outside. Looking around, I nervously went in to find out what had happened.

The elderly dealer had been badly roughed up and apparently had had a slight stroke. I felt responsible for this tragedy and spoke to his business partner about the photographs. He couldn't give me much more information, except that they were from a deceased estate he believed to be from the village of Lavington. He thought it more likely to be Market Lavington and not West Lavington.

The Police Sergeant came over to me and asked, 'What's your interest in this, sir?' with a rather suspicious tone.

'I came in this morning and bought an old photograph,' I replied calmly, 'and the old gentleman said he might have another one for me, so I returned at the time he suggested.'

'Do you have the old photograph with you?' he said. 'Yes, I have', I said, taking it out carefully and unwrapping it. Fortunately the receipt was also in the small parcel.

'Ah,' he said slowly, looking at it carefully, 'and what is it?'

'It's a Daguerreotype, an early type of French photograph, late 19th century – a prized collectors' item.'

He seemed satisfied with my answer, after taking my name and address and the fact that I was staying at the Bear Hotel in the town. 'Thank you. Where are you from?' he continued, seemingly just making polite conversation as the ambulance officers attended to the sick man. 'I'm from Tasmania, Australia. Touring around Southern England – just a tourist, you might say.'

'This is a sad business,' I continued. 'He is a notable expert on antiques, I believe.'

'Yes,' said the policeman, 'but he is going to be alright though, according to the ambulance people. They came very promptly and treated him immediately, thanks to his partner dialling for the ambulance so quickly. He should have retired. Perhaps he will now after all this.'

The business partner strolled across to me and stood by my side as we closely watched the stretcher being carried out to the ambulance. He waited till the police had gone and then said to me, 'This is a really bad thing! What the hell is going on in the world? As I came into the shop,' he continued, 'I could hear raised voices and as two men rushed out past me I realised my partner had been badly hurt and collapsed. I went in to help him rather than try to stop them, which I couldn't do anyway.'

'You told the police, I assume?' I asked with hesitation.

'Yes, but I couldn't give them much of a description. Dark suits, tall and rather swarthy looking.'

I murmured something non-committal and said, 'Thank you.' However I was quite certain who they were.

Disappointed, I left the shop and started walking towards the town centre and the hotel and suddenly the Austin was coming up the street quickly towards me. The friendly bar attendant wound down the window and shouted something which, because of his broad Wiltshire accent I didn't quite understand.

'Get in quick!' he shouted louder. That I clearly understood and took a flying leap into the back seat of the car.

'What the flaming hell is going on?' he said angrily. I started to try to explain again, but he didn't listen.

'Well, I don't like it. The car is bloody fantastic, but I must get home to Potterne to rest for my next spell at the hotel. Do you realise those stupid bastards tried to run me off the road? You're not telling me the whole truth – are you? And you used me in some mad crazy scheme!'

I thought for a minute as we went into the town centre and said, 'It's better if you know nothing. It's far too dangerous. I'm sorry I put you in possible danger. Play dumb, say nothing if you should cross their paths again. I will explain at a later date when – and if – I return.'

'Stay down in the back!' he yelled suddenly. 'OK, stay calm,' I answered and followed his instructions. At that moment a car passed us. 'I'll drive the car a different way to Potterne and then you can go on to wherever you like – on your own.'

'But how will you get back to the hotel?' I asked. 'No problem. I can catch a lift, taxi or bus. I'll be alright. You're into something crazy – I really don't want to be part of it! I'll put you on the right road. Then you're on your own.'

He turned the car round in a wildly exaggerated movement to show off his driving skills. Potterne was a pleasant village with an amazing old porch house from medieval times, he explained proudly.

I drove the car to Market Lavington in a leisurely and careful manner, keeping a watchful eye. I saw a sign which told me the Village Fair was coming very soon, with bunting, flags and balloons festooned everywhere. Not knowing exactly where to start looking, I stopped outside the village shop and going inside, I bought a local newspaper.

I indicated a rather tasty looking pie to the shopkeeper and was about to ask what was in it, when a calm voice spoke by the side of me. 'It's a locally produced apple pie, the very best of course.' I thanked him for his help, bought it and went out into the street.

The man followed me out and walked by my side. 'You're not local, are you?' he said.

'No, not really,' I replied. 'Just a tourist looking for and photographing old buildings and especially interesting churches.' His interest seemed to focus immediately.

'Well, you've met the right man. My name is Paul Charlton. I'm not an expert, of course, on church architecture, but I am the Vicar of this Parish. They call me The Rev, short for the Reverend,' he explained with a grin. 'The parish church is St Mary's.'

'Pleased to meet you, Paul. My name's Jack Harrison,' I replied warmly.

I had no reason to disbelieve him, although he wasn't wearing a dog collar. He noticed my surprise as we walked down the High Street. I really felt I could trust him, so I told him briefly about my quest and my interest in old photographs and calligraphy. 'Perhaps you would like to join my wife Carolyn and me for afternoon tea? I can tell you more about the history of the village,' he said, with increasing enthusiasm.

We went into his small Georgian house in the High Street and he introduced me to his charming wife, who soon made afternoon tea and invited me to join them in friendly conversation, which was most enjoyable. I also learnt that there was a small museum in the village that could give me all the possible information I could desire about the long history of the village, even from before Roman times.

The two of them were interesting and excellent talkers and obviously enjoyed talking to a perfect stranger. They told me about a past rector of the church called Bishop Tanner who was a well known person in the village and also a great collector and writer of books – in other words, an amateur archivist and antiquarian. This was the sort of information I was seeking – perhaps I might be getting somewhere. Perhaps Bishop Tanner was the key to my final objective. I was surprised and excited with this unexpected turn of events.

'Tell me everything you know about him,' I said, 'especially about his books and documents and what happened to them.'

I listened very carefully as he recounted the history. 'Thomas Tanner was born in this village in 1674 and went to Queens College, Oxford.'

Paul and his wife were very knowledgeable and knew much about the history of Bishop Tanner and the village. 'The Bishop was an antiquarian and a great collector and writer,' he continued, obviously enjoying his subject. 'Upon his death in 1735 his valuable and most interesting books and manuscripts were sent to the Bodleian Library at Oxford, but almost didn't make it. As he was the Bishop of St Asaph some papers might also be there.'

'What happened?' I said, rather concerned, hoping they weren't damaged.

'There was an accident with the barge on the way to Oxford via the River Thames, or so the story goes, but almost all were saved, although we can't be sure. He might have taken some to St Asaph in 1732, three years before he died in Oxford.'

'Where is St Asaph? I have never heard of it'

'It's in Denbighshire in North Wales,' he replied. 'It's a beautiful mountainous area, and of course near Mt Snowdon and Portmeirion. We are both keen hikers, so we visited quite a lot of North Wales, plus the beautiful Lake District which is also within two hours driving. Both areas are within easy drive of Liverpool where I was a young priest. It was a tough city with many problems, but I live in hope that we helped the youths in my parish. Believe it or not I taught them the noble art of boxing – or tried to.'

This information was truly of great help and I realised that my quest could be on the right track at last.

'May I ask if there were any manuscripts left in the village here?' I said quietly in hope.

'Rather doubtful,' he replied, shaking his head. 'Most probably they all went to the Bodleian Library, but maybe some items were left behind at St Asaph Cathedral in North Wales.'

I knew I was getting close, but once again the elusive pages seemed to be slipping from my grasp. There was only one thing to do and that was to go to St Asaph Cathedral first thing in the morning and keep ahead of my pursuers. So I explained my mission to them in more detail.

'Well, best of luck for tomorrow. Early start for you I guess. My wife Carolyn will make you a solid breakfast after you have had a good night's rest.' I thanked him for his kind friendship and hospitality.

CHAPTER 8

HEREFORD TO ST ASAPH

I set off eagerly the next morning, loaded with enough food provided by Carolyn the Vicar's wife, a route map to Wales and a detailed map of North Wales, a flask of tea and their good wishes. I asked them not to mention this to anyone in the village until I returned, hopefully triumphant.

I was now more confident of success, but also wary of the pitfalls of overconfidence. Instead of going through Devizes again, I went through the countryside towards Marlborough and picked up the motorway just south of Swindon, travelling towards the River Severn and following the motorway which kept north of Bristol. I crossed the River Severn and reached Chepstow in very good time.

The car was running beautifully, the weather was good and the countryside fresh, lush and green. Deciding to stop at Monmouth and check the fuel, oil and water and believing I was making good time, I noted the distance and estimated my time of arrival in Hereford City. Did I have time to visit the 14th century Cathedral and the famous Mappa Mundi and the Chained Library? It was very tempting for a keen student of calligraphy and I mulled over the prospect.

I decided to have a bite to eat near the Cathedral where I could at least see the medieval city. The Chained Library was of particular interest to me because of the calligraphy connection and its fascinating history, but sadly I decided I could not stay because of lack of time.

The Rev had told me a little about the Cathedral and its history, so I parked the car near Bridge Street, took my bag, camera, picnic lunch and strolled towards the grassed area around the Cathedral where I sat down in the shade. It was a tranquil setting which lulled me into a relaxed and calm state of mind. Waking with a start, I realised I had dozed off, so I stretched my limbs, got up, took a few photographs and finished the meal. I went back to the Austin and negotiated my way through Hereford, keeping to the A49 and driving north for a while. I realised after a time I was confused with my map reading, but I kept going because North Wales was my target, i.e. due north.

Unfamiliar with the area, I slowed down slightly to check the map. Coming to a bend still looking for somewhere to stop safely, I caught sight of something that made my heart jump. Two cars were blocking the way across the road, their bonnets pointing in a V-shape towards my car.

I braked slightly and considered what to do. I rammed the car into second gear and accelerated very hard, and then into third, still increasing speed. The three figures were now beginning to panic and moving quickly to get out of their cars. I spun the wheel and pulled hard on the handbrake.

The car now had a mind of its own and spun round, having slipped on wet mud or leaves, and was travelling backwards very fast. It crashed into the two cars, locking them firmly together and in such a way that it would take some time to get untangled.

Although the old Austin was severely crumpled at the back and the lid was flapping up and down, I drove off in the opposite direction, but managed to keep going by using plenty of engine revs. My handbrake turn was not well executed – it wasn't perfect, but it did the trick. I had learned that manoeuvre as part of my basic training in the Department in London and I'd done it in early practice, but never for real.

The engine was decidedly loud and sounded rough. The exhaust pipe was obviously broken, so I pulled off the road into a field, crashed through the farm gate which was conveniently half open, a definite 'no-no' in farming circles, but I was grateful.

Travelling across the hayfield I made a bee-line for the far side of a hayrick to hide the car. The engine was now making so much noise it didn't sound at all good, and so I cut the engine and leapt out to check the extent of the damage. The manifold and exhaust pipe had come adrift, part of Dan Cooper's impressive handiwork – he wouldn't be happy.

While looking at the engine and wondering what to do, I noticed a little metal box which of course was a transmitter – I should have checked more carefully. They must have put it in the engine bay in Devizes outside the Bear Hotel. It was magnetic and had become dislodged in the crash and lay there on the sump guard. I picked it up and put it in my pocket for some reason without thinking clearly.

In the distance I could hear the two cars racing towards me. I grabbed my bag, camera and remaining food and sprinted like the wind for the far side of the field and dived through the hawthorn hedge, cutting my hand in doing so. I reached the other side of the hedge before they entered the field and was able to watch them unseen.

I watched in dismay as they riddled the car with bullets out of sheer moronic stupidity, or blind rage, possibly believing that I was still in the car. The result was predictable – suddenly the petrol tank, which they must have hit, started leaking fuel and the car was engulfed in flames with a loud explosion, also setting fire to the hayrick.

Clutching my gear I hobbled along behind the hedge, keeping well down, onto the road and started limping in a northerly direction to get away from the scene, while they were occupied with the magnificent pyrotechnics.

I was walking with difficulty, because when I had dived through the hedge my ankle twisted and I couldn't run. Several cars passed me as I tried to thumb a lift. I now had no car and the sun was going down; black clouds were starting to form in the distant hills.

I had no idea what to do next. My Italian coat was only shower proof. Things didn't look good. The road was unknown to me, in the middle of the wilds of Wales. Finally it was about to rain heavily, my food supply was low and I was tired and hungry. It was rather depressing to say the least and the temperature was now dropping sharply.

Another car was approaching, travelling fast as the driver changed gears very skilfully, so I stuck my thumb out hopefully. But it went past me. Then it screeched to a halt and waited while I limped as quickly as I could towards it. I couldn't believe my luck. The driver leaned across and opened the passenger door and a female voice shouted, 'Get in! Quick!'

I didn't hesitate, but followed her instructions, with great difficulty because my ankle was still painful. Realising it was a young woman, which was more startling, I thanked her and introduced myself, explaining that my car had broken down.

'That's a bit of an understatement,' she said with a slight laugh. 'Was that blazing car and hayrick your handiwork?'

'I'm afraid so. They riddled the poor old Austin with bullets and set fire to it, which then set fire to the hayrick.'

I glanced backwards and the sky was now glowing orange and red. The fire was out of control and could be seen for miles. 'It was my friend's car. He will be, to say the least, very angry. I assured him I'd take good care of it.'

'Well, you have certainly broken your promise,' she replied, with no humour in her voice.

I agreed. 'He is a good friend, and he offered to take my hire car back to London as well.'

'Oh dear Lord, you're in serious trouble,' she said solemnly.

I glanced at her sideways to discern what sort of woman would pick up an unknown dishevelled stranger in the wilds of mid-Wales. The glow from the instrument panel showed her to have a controlled look on her face, but whether that was due to concentrating on her driving or not, I didn't know. She was elegantly dressed and looked very attractive. I could not believe my good luck yet again – what kind of Good Samaritan was this attractive young lady who had summed up the situation in a glance and decided to trust me?

She sensed the question on my mind and said, 'I saw you in the gloom. Then I noticed your hand was bleeding. Your face is an awful mess too. We must get you cleaned up when we get to my hotel. And by the way, you smell awful, like a farmyard.'

I apologised to her most profusely as we sped along the country road, and I told her about my frantic dive through the hedge. The mere mention of a hotel made me feel much better. 'You're very kind,' I murmured. Do you know this road very well?'

'Yes, North Wales is one of my favourite places. I'm a photographer, mostly architectural buildings. But I qualified in architecture at Bristol University which is where I live now, in an apartment with a girlfriend.' That answered my next question – probably not married.

'Are you married?' she asked tentatively, obviously reading my mind.

'No, sadly not. I did have a fiancée once, but because of my work it all fell apart.'

'Your work was what – exactly?' she asked.

'Well, I always seemed to be travelling and never there with her, irregular hours and so on, not much of a relationship for her.'

'No, of course! Some women need the company. You still didn't answer my question,' she replied.

'I didn't, did I? Very rude of me. I'm sorry. It's rather involved and complicated.'

'Sounds intriguing, even mysterious,' she replied.

I stopped and thought for a few seconds. Should I tell her the truth or not? Changing the subject, I said, 'I was actually going to St Asaph or at least the Cathedral which might have some old manuscripts. I'm a keen amateur calligrapher you see, and I do mean amateur.'

There was a moment's pause and then she said, 'I'm going to Portmeirion which is not far away, to take photographs for an article I am doing for a Sunday paper. They pay very well for illustrated articles. Perhaps I could do one on St Asaph as well?'

Thoughtfully I realised that might solve my problem. 'Good idea. Have you heard of a Thomas Tanner who was Bishop of St Asaph in the 18th century. He was an author, collector and antiquarian. His valuable books and manuscripts are now in the Bodleian Library, in Oxford.'

'Well, that sounds like another possibility for an interesting article,' she replied.

I thought, how incredible it would be if this all came together satisfactorily. It now seemed possible once again.

The conversation flagged so I said, 'You didn't tell me your name?'

'Fiona Ballantyne,' she replied. 'Have you heard the name or seen any of my articles?'

'No, because I live in Tasmania now, at least for the last two and a half years.'

'How extraordinary!' she said. 'Why Tasmania?'

'It's a long and complicated story, which I will tell you later perhaps, when we have more time,' I said.

'You are making me very curious. I love Italic writing too. I can do calligraphy, but not very well. No, I haven't heard of Bishop Tanner. I'm glad I stopped to pick you up, you're a rather interesting man,' she said thoughtfully.

'Thanks for that. I am most grateful you did. You can't believe how grateful,' I said, thinking about the serious trouble I was in.

Conversation dried up for a moment or two and then she said, 'You said that was your friend's car back there that set light to the hayrick?'

'Yes, it was. You might think it was an extreme act of stupidity by them. I must warn you that these are dangerous people who are chasing me.'

'Well, that's given me a few clues to make an informed guess,' she said thoughtfully.

I had chatted on about my situation, but without great detail. Nevertheless, she had a quick mind and had pieced things together. She definitely wasn't slow on the uptake and it was clear she was used to making quick judgements. Watching her out of the corner of my eye, I was impressed with her competent driving, moving smoothly through the manual gearbox along the winding roads.

Suddenly the engine coughed and then continued. She changed down a gear and tried again and then carried on driving, but the engine died altogether and went silent. We coasted to a halt. I got out and looked along the road; there was a big shed nearby, so we pushed it down onto the farm track and into the implement shed, which was open and had farm machinery and bales of hay inside. There was just enough space for us to push the car in and close the double doors.

With daylight almost gone, I took off my top coat and got to work on the car, checking everything possible, but without success. It was a rear engine sports car, which was not my best field of expertise. She looked at me with a grim smile, but said nothing and then magically produced two car rugs from the car. We then put bales of hay between the closed shed doors and the rear of the car to cut down any wind and to give us some insulation, and also to hide us visually if the farmer should open the doors.

All this was done almost silently, with hardly a word from either of us. We seemed to think as one, but I was also turning over in my mind what was the problem with the car. We put the adjustable seats back as far as they would go and settled down to sleep as best we could. It wasn't the best night's sleep, but it had to do for now.

The Smallest Cathedral

The morning came and I opened the car door as quietly as possible without waking Fiona. I looked at her and she was sleeping very soundly. I also realised how very attractive she was.

I surveyed the shed in search of any available tools. The old Ferguson tractor held some promise, but no luck, because the tools were only suitable for farming equipment. I peeped out of the back window of the shed and saw a water tank at the rear. Although it was freezing cold at that time of the morning, I stripped off to my waist and washed. There was no mirror of course, so I was unable to see my face.

Suddenly a female voice called out, 'I have a small mirror which might help you.' Fiona came round the corner and looked at me with concern. 'You're a mess Jack, have a look at yourself. There's dried blood in your hair mixed with mud – let me help you.' After she had finished, I had a look in the mirror and felt and looked much better.

We had another look in the engine bay. I inspected the air cleaner and cleaned the filter out, placing it away from the car. I then started the car up again, it fired briefly and then stopped.

This time Fiona turned the ignition, but again it went very unevenly and stopped. I then swapped two of the leads over and the engine fired up again. There was a mild explosion, but it stopped again after running very roughly. 'Now we're getting somewhere,' I said, looking at Fiona hopefully.

'That's good?' she said, questioning me.

'Yes, I think I know what it is – it's the fuel filter, or dirty fuel. Where is the fuel filter?'

She looked at me and raised her hands in the manner of: 'I really don't know,' and smiled.

'I'm certain that's the problem – we've checked everything else. So it must be that,' I replied.

After searching for several minutes, I found the fuel line and the filter. It was in an awkward place underneath the car. Fiona had to clean me up once again. I re-assembled everything correctly and turned the ignition on – it ran smoothly and we were soon moving again.

'I'm starving,' she said suddenly, 'how about you? It's only about an hour's drive to St Asaph in Denbighshire.'

'Great idea, although we should buy a fuel filter. I don't trust my temporary repair.'

I watched her confident driving; she obviously knew the roads very well.

'We can eat while they fix the car,' she said brightly.

'If you can get someone to do it in this area, that would be time saving all round. But can you?'

'Well, I know a young mechanic who is very helpful and will remember me,' she replied.

We managed to reach Denbigh without any more trouble. We pulled into the garage where a young good looking man came out, saw Fiona and greeted her warmly.

'Hallo! Miss Ballantyne, nice to see you again. How can I help?'

Fiona, with great charm and feminine persuasion, asked him to change the fuel filter while we had a much needed breakfast. It was a smooth piece of talking, I thought. He was obviously charmed by her beauty and feminine approach.

While they were talking, I put my hand in my pocket and took out the tracking device and studied it while I sat in the car. If it was still working, which I presumed it was, I had to put it on another car which, hopefully, would be travelling in another direction. I had made a stupid error in keeping it. It now put both of us in danger.

I walked across the road and spoke to a gentleman sitting in his car queuing for fuel and asked him if it was far to Cardiff from here. He wasn't quite sure, but thought it about three hours. The answer didn't really matter, because while we were talking I attached the unwanted tracking device inside the front wheel arch.

'Are you travelling south from here?' I said.

'Yes, we are going to Hereford to see the Cathedral.'

'Oh good,' I said, 'make sure you see the Mappa Mundi and the Chained Library, it's terrific.'

'That's exactly what we are going for,' he said with enthusiasm. 'Many thanks.'

I wished him well and crossed the road to Fiona, who was now finishing her coffee in one of those awful cardboard cups.

'What on earth were you doing over there?' she said, rather curiously.

'Nothing much, we were just chatting about cars.'

'That was an old Austin 1800 like the one you had, wasn't it?'

'Yes, correct,' I said. She had noticed much more than I had realised – very little escaped her keen eye. It certainly would not fool them entirely, but it might confuse them for a short while.

While I was eating a rather scrappy but much needed breakfast, Fiona visited the ladies and made herself 'presentable' as she called it. She came out looking very smart, with her face made up and fresh lipstick.

'You better go and clean up too,' she advised. 'You're still a bit scruffy. Here. Borrow my comb.'

Looking in the mirror was a nasty shock. She was right. As I came out she greeted me with the information that my elderly gentleman had moved off. At that moment one of the cars that had caused me to stop last evening, turned round in the road and followed. I turned my head swiftly and went back into the gentlemen's toilet, hoping I wouldn't be seen. It was a close call. Obviously the tracking device was working, but it would be easy for them to work out that I had tricked them, if only for a short time.

'I'm ready to go. Are you?' I whispered.

'Yes, I'm now very behind schedule, because of you and the car problem. Portmeirion is waiting. I didn't have an exact time but I want to get the morning light and shadows just right.'

The little red MG sports car came down off the hoist and Fiona paid. He warned her to keep an eye on the fuel filter in future. She thanked him and gave him a hug. He smiled and said, 'It's been a pleasure, Miss Ballantyne.'

'Now I know why you stopped here at Denbigh,' I said, 'instead of going straight to St Asaph.' I grinned in a friendly way.

'Don't get the wrong idea,' she said, laughing.

'Well, what's all this "Miss Ballantyne"? Yes and no Miss Ballantyne, three bags full Miss Ballantyne!'

'I told you not to get the wrong idea. He's my cheeky cousin, and it's his way of chiding me for not being married,' she replied, chuckling with laughter.

'Ah, I understand now. Well, we'd better move quickly.'

It took us no time at all to get to St Asaph where Fiona knew a good bed and breakfast place to stay. She went off immediately to Portmeirion to take her photographs and I was left to explore the cathedral town. It was very compact and contains the smallest cathedral in England and Wales, but it could possibly contain an immense treasure for me in the Cathedral Museum.

It didn't take me long to find the Dean, who once again was fascinated by my story, but sadly didn't think there was much chance of locating anything of value, or even a small clue. Nevertheless, he was happy to let me search.

'Let me introduce you to our fascinating collection of old prayer books and Bibles, which includes the remarkable *Breeches and Vinegar Bible*, as it's called.' He explained the text to me by opening the Bible at the right page and explained every thing about its strange history.

'Do you think Bishop Tanner saw these Bibles?' I asked hopefully.

'I'm sure he did. In fact, I believe he was responsible for assembling a part of this little collection. So you know about Bishop Tanner, do you?'

'Yes I do. He was born in Market Lavington, Wiltshire,' I replied.

The Dean looked at me, surprised at my knowledge, and said, 'I don't think there is anything here, but there might be a small clue or a page with handwritten notes. Let's look for that. It will take a couple of days, because we will have to be slow and careful to protect the fragile documents. There are about 2000 items here,' he said proudly.

We searched meticulously through the collection and were somewhere about mid-morning when he found a note signed by Thomas Tanner. 'Have a look at this,' he said, passing the tiny document over. 'It's written in Latin. How's your Latin?'

'First year only,' I replied. 'I can remember *agricola* is a farmer, and other odd words, but not much else.'

He smiled and said, 'Only religious Latin for me, I'm afraid. I'll take it away and get out my college books, or speak to a colleague. Tomorrow it will have to be. I have some duties to perform for the Cathedral now. Hope you won't mind, but I must finish.'

I nodded assent and we agreed to meet again at ten o'clock the next day. He did advise me where I could get a good meal at a reasonable price – in the local pub.

After the pub meal I went back to the B&B and got a quick nap, but before that I once again thought about how my search had panned out, and my juggernaut journey half way around the globe from my farm in Tasmania.

Having left in such a hurry, I realised I had left things in a bit of a mess for Peter Morris and Nick. I had been chased, captured, beaten up, incarcerated in Venice and nearly burned alive in Dan Cooper's automotive masterpiece. Now into the equation comes Fiona, who has thrown me into a state of emotional conflict.

Was it pure chance she came along at that time; or was she following some instruction or direction perhaps from Loader? Was she really a photographic journalist, or was that just a cover? How could I be sure of anyone? Only time will tell, or should I ask her outright when she returned from Portmeirion?

When we were at Denbigh she seemed to move across in front of me almost naturally; or was it a pure accident. If so, did she know more about my quest than she was saying? This was hardly likely, as it would be so simple just to say Loader had sent her to join me. Yet she seemed to take it all in her stride as if expecting it. She was undoubtedly a bright, intelligent young woman who didn't seem to be put out by the old Austin being shot up and burnt. As soon as I could find the opportunity, I should ring Peter Morris in Tasmania and tell him that negotiations were going well.

I nodded off to sleep. The night's sleep in a cold barn had not been at all comfortable, so I took every opportunity catch up on my sleep.

Eventually I awoke and thought about Fiona and wondered how she was getting along with her enterprise. I hoped that when she returned I would have something positive to tell her. The B&B people provided me with a superb evening meal, so I retired early to get some more needed rest.

The following morning at nine o'clock I went straight to the Cathedral and met the Dean who seemed to be excited with his investigations.

'Well,' he started, 'I was a bit puzzled by this *M.L.* reference, which I took to be a Latin date at first, but it transpires that it is referring to that village you mentioned in Wiltshire – Market Lavington. It says here in Thomas Tanner's original script and the translation that there must be still some valuable pages at the village, which the Bishop thought could be most interesting and needed comparing with the original pages of the *Book of Kells* or others of a similar period.' Did the Bishop write in Latin for secrecy?

Once again my hopes rose and then fell and I mentioned that I had been to Market Lavington and drawn a blank. He looked at me nonplussed, not knowing what to say. He then brightened up and said.

'Cheer up! We're not even halfway through the collection, there might be another clue for us.' So we continued searching carefully until lunchtime and I went off to the pub again, keeping to the small side streets to avoid being seen.

Our afternoon session went very well; the Dean was in a good mood and enthusiastic. We handled the books and documents carefully, but found little of help. We were having a great time and didn't lose any of our fervour for the job in hand.

'Have a look at this,' he said suddenly, passing over another note from an old book. 'This one is signed and dated but thank goodness it's written in English and refers to his *Notitia Monastica*, which is the book that Bishop Tanner published in Oxford in 1695. It also refers to his other book *Bibliotecca Britannica – Hibernica*, a dictionary of authors of the 17th century and before.'

This was starting to become interesting and exhilarating. Surely, we thought, there must be a clue here somewhere. The Bishop's two books were now almost certainly at the Bodleian Library in Oxford, but there was no reference to the missing pages. Sadly, we'd found nothing by the end of the day. Even so, we parted in good spirits and I said that I was unsure whether I would come back the next day.

'Remember young man, I will always be here for you. I will continue searching now that you have ignited my interest,' he replied with a gracious smile. He gave me his card with a telephone number to ring if I needed to call him about anything else.

I was thinking about Fiona again, wondering how her project was progressing. I was eager to tell her my news, although I still had nothing definite. I went back to the B&B, slept well and woke the next morning in a positive frame of mind.

I was enjoying a good solid English breakfast which I had almost finished, when Fiona burst into the breakfast room, strode purposefully across the room, kissed me on the forehead and whispered in my ear, 'Your unpleasant friends are here darling. We really ought to go.'

I muttered something nasty under my breath as she grabbed my toast and marmalade. We walked out of the breakfast room as calmly as possible. She paid the bill while I retrieved my bag and coat from the bedroom.

'How do you know it's them?' I muttered quietly in the hallway.

'Well, there are two big limousines just down the street with severely damaged front ends, so I guessed it was them. My car is round the back. You get into it and stay there until I come back to you. As soon as they move off, we'll go in the other direction, back to Bristol.'

There was no time to ask questions, so I followed her plan. I waited nearly five nervous minutes hiding in the car.

'The tank is full so we are going back to Bristol,' she said firmly when she returned to me.

'What's your plan? And why Bristol anyway?' I said.

'My apartment is in Bristol and from here, there's a dozen ways of getting there. Besides, I know the route well, so sit back and relax for a pleasant scenic ride.'

She was right about her knowledge of the roads. We led them a merry dance, going from minor roads to main roads and motorway. We eventually lost them. Her driving as usual was admirable and that certain question came into my mind again —¬ was she really a photographic- journalist? So I said, 'Where is your camera? I'm keen to see photographs of Portmeirion.'

'When we reach Bristol you can see them, but at the moment they are in a special metal compartment behind your seat. With expensive equipment such as that, I can't take the risk of having them stolen,' she explained.

That satisfied my curiosity, so I let the matter rest. As we weaved our way through Wales and back into England, I rang the Dean of St Asaph on Fiona's mobile and he assured me that he was certain the missing pages – if they existed at all – were at Market Lavington. The Dean had found another note, clearly in Bishop Tanner's writing. He had written to ask that the pages which he was so keen on, should come to St Asaph's collection, because he believed they were most valuable. The Dean reminded me again that he hadn't finished searching through the over two thousand volumes, manuscripts and pages, but he would continue searching. I thanked him most warmly.

Another question came into my mind: How was it that they spotted Fiona's car in Portmeirion? 'By the way, is the car registered in Bristol? Or where?' I said casually.

'No, it's a London registration,' she said, 'because that's our Head Office. Why do you ask?'

'Because if they know your car is registered in Bristol they will make for Bristol in the hope of spotting us. But London's a much bigger city and it would be more difficult to find us.'

'I see what you mean. But how will they find that out, supposing that they have our number plate?' she said.

'I have a suspicion that there is someone else with influence, higher above them in the organisation. Someone we have not yet seen, who is directing these three or four thugs who just take orders. Quite who is directing them I still don't know. It's not at all clear.'

We journeyed through the countryside until we reached the city of Bath, the original old Roman settlement, then on to Bristol and Fiona's apartment in Leigh Woods which looked luxurious. 'So this is how a successful photographer lives, is it?' I said with a grin.

'Yes, I love it here. It's a good spot for my work. I have research to do on the computer tonight, but let's have a meal first. I'm famished. What would you like to eat?'

'Anything you produce will be fine I'm sure,' I said politely and enthusiastically. She went into the kitchen asking me if I would like a drink of wine.

I enjoyed a sherry. I then thought I should acquaint her with more information about my search and my trip across the world, my visit to the Vatican Library in Rome. I left out some of the details of my incarceration in Venice. She was keen to hear my story while she was cooking, and we sat down to an excellent meal and exchanged details about our work.

The sleeping arrangements were simple, I slept in her bed and she slept in her flatmate Kate's bedroom, because Kate and her fiancé were away for the night.

I slept solidly, but the following morning I awoke to experience something I hadn't quite expected. There was a faint but unmistakeable aroma of a woman's expensive perfume. I turned over slowly and looked surprised at Fiona in the bed next to me. 'What happened?' I said half awake.

'Don't worry,' Fiona said, 'nothing happened. Kate and Alan came back a day early after you had gone to bed, so I must have misunderstood what Kate told me. Or got the dates wrong.'

'I have lost track of the days too, it's been hectic,' I said in agreement. She slowly leaned down and kissed me on the forehead. 'There, is that better?' And then kissed me on the lips. I replied by returning her kiss and now, being fully awake and exchanging caresses, we made love.

We lay there in the warmth and glow of our bodies, just smiling and holding each other closely. I pulled the bedclothes over us, which was just as well because there was a sharp knock on the door and a female face looked in and said, 'Oh, sorry to interrupt,' and swiftly closed the door again. Fiona giggled, turned over and started to get out of bed and swiftly dressed, so I did the same.

At breakfast, we all sat in the very modern kitchen around the breakfast bar, but I kept getting inquisitive glances from Kate and Alan. Fiona noticed this and told them I was a calligrapher from Tasmania, which wasn't quite accurate, but it satisfied their curiosity briefly.

There was a pause in the conversation, and then Kate said, 'Do you make much money as a calligrapher?'

'No, not much, but I have other avenues of making money,' I said blithely. I knew this sounded pompous and likely to lead to further questions, so Fiona interrupted swiftly.

'He's researching the *Book of Kells* and we might go to Dublin to do further work.'

I was sorry she had mentioned Dublin because of the *Book of Kells*, but it seemed upon reflection a good idea. Anyway, I said to them, 'It would be just as well if you didn't mention this to anyone, because Fiona and I are writing an illustrated book on Dublin and the history of the famous book.' This they seemed to understand and thought it a brilliant idea.

'By the way Fiona, did you have much luck at Portmeirion?' Kate asked.

'Oh yes, a fabulous day, the light was perfect. Come and see them on the computer.'

We all crowded around the computer with suitably admiring comments. They were excellent. 'I sent them off to London last night,' she said, 'so they should be in the paper next weekend.'

Fiona suggested we go and see Brunel's famous suspension bridge. She was very knowledgeable about Brunel the great 19th century engineer, and wanted to show me her favourite bridge. I was very keen on him myself and didn't want to cramp her enthusiasm. I said that I must make a few phone calls and would catch up later, but in reality I wanted to ring the Dean at St Asaph, and the Reverend Charlton in Wiltshire. I was also concerned about Loader. However, my first call was to Peter Morris in Tasmania, having checked the time difference carefully. He, like most farmers, went to bed early, so my timing had to be precise.

'Hallo, Peter speaking. How can I help?' he answered.

'Hallo Peter, it's Jack ringing from England.'

'Is it? Well, I'll be blowed,' and there then followed the usual Australian expletives, as he told me about Loader.

'I went to visit him to check him out as you suggested, and he seemed to be OK and making good progress. Then the missus went in with flowers, fruit and a good book, which he was happy with. Then the third time I went in, he had gone! Buggered off without any explanation. The staff weren't happy either, because he didn't tell them anything. For that matter, he didn't say anything to me that made much sense either.'

I thought how typical of Loader to slip away like that.

'Peter, it's alright. Don't worry. I owe you an apology, an explanation. And thanks for everything you've done.'

'What about a bit of clarification?' he said firmly.

'Well, I didn't tell you the entire truth and I shouldn't. Not yet anyway. But I will when I return,' I replied.

'And when will that be?' he said quickly.

'Still unsure. But we are making good progress. How's the farm? And Nick too?' trying to change the subject.

'I've put one man there sort of permanently. I hope you don't mind? As for Nick, he runs around the place looking for you, sniffing at everything.'

'I don't mind at all, so don't worry. I trust your judgement completely, Peter.'

I then rang the Dean at St Asaph and explained my hasty exit, and why. He told me that he had found more information about Wiltshire and that he felt absolutely certain the missing pages were there. This was really good news. But where were they? It didn't add up, so I rang the Reverend and told him that the Dean was so sure the pages were in the village. This puzzled the Reverend slightly, because he had searched the Church and the Vicarage thoroughly; even upstairs in the loft and the basement.

I was getting nowhere and fighting off a slight headache. Fiona then came back with Alan and Kate from their visit to the Clifton Suspension Bridge. She was a little shaken up by the fact that she thought she had seen one of the black cars from mid-Wales, but it turned out to be a false alarm. Although it was the same model, it didn't have the tell-tale damage from my deliberate crash.

'Well, let's have another look at the Portmeirion photographs, shall we.'

Fiona started the computer up and went to her latest photographs. But now I became very interested, because the first one showed a familiar face, one that I didn't want to see – it was that of the ugly character I thumped in Venice, still with a plaster on his nose. He was only in the top right hand corner of the photograph but just visible. It was definitely him. I was now concerned for Fiona who had become drawn into this affair, but I made no comment.

'Oh damn, sorry, something I completely forgot,' she said suddenly, grabbing a national paper and opening it so I could see the article about the old Austin. It was headlined, 'Odd mystery in Mid Wales' and ended with the words, 'but no body was found in the burnt out wreck.'

'Oh hell!' I said. 'I'll have to tell Dick Cooper eventually. I wasn't going to enjoy telling Dick what the truth really was. I finally rang him reluctantly.

When Dick heard my voice he answered angrily, and a load of bad language followed. Finally, he calmed down a bit and said, 'The police have been here because of the number plate and questioned me, but I couldn't tell them anything, as I don't know where you are. You really are a damn pain in the neck, Jack!' he said.

'Dick I'm sorry. It wasn't my fault. These bastards are very dangerous and have no respect for people or property.' I slammed the phone down quickly, just in case the police were tapping his phone for information. I determined then that Loader would pay for the car at least, and possibly the farmers' hayrick.

I had now rung everyone I should and had come to a dead end, so Fiona and I sat down to a simple meal and discussed what to do next. She was, of course, still keen to go to Dublin, but I dissuaded her by saying that at this stage it could be dangerous. She wasn't entirely happy with this answer so I explained that I wanted to go too, but only at the end of the quest when we had found the missing pages.

This seemed to make her happy because she was keen to write an illustrated article on the *Book of Kells*. Finally, after much thought, we decided to go to the Bodleian Library in Oxford the next day, and went to bed early.

CHAPTER 10

TO OXFORD (BODLEIAN LIBRARY)

The following morning we set off extremely early, before dawn, to avoid being seen. Fiona and I borrowed Harry's car, which was a concern, because it was almost brand new and he had not had it long, but he was mollified by Fiona who offered him her MG sports car in exchange. We took the M4 motorway, which at that time of the morning was comparatively free of traffic, and arrived very early in Oxford, found a café, had a quick breakfast and ambled through Oxford towards the Bodleian Library.

As the library opened its doors, we were the first people at the entrance. We approached the counter and I asked to speak to Professor Thomas Watson-Young. The gentleman behind the counter looked at us with a surprised look. 'The Professor doesn't see anybody without an appointment' he said, rather stiffly.

'Yes, of course, I understand,' I replied. 'However, I have a letter of introduction from a Mr Loader, of the British Government.'

'Ah I see. Please wait here for a few minutes and I will see if he is available.'

Fiona and I exchanged anxious glances while we waited. He returned after a few minutes and took us to the Professor's room and ushered us in. The Professor looked very distinguished and smiled. 'How can I help you?' he said quietly.

I explained the situation to him briefly and he nodded. 'May I see the letter of introduction please?'

I took the letter out of my inside pocket and immediately realised something was wrong. The envelope was addressed to the Professor but there didn't seem to be much paper in it. I handed it over anyway. He studied the slip of paper and then carefully held it up to the light. Fiona looked as puzzled as I, and we looked at the distinguished man, who then smiled warmly at us.

'You must be Mr Harrison,' he said swiftly.

'Yes, quite correct,' I replied, 'and this is my friend and associate, Fiona Ballantyne, a photographic journalist.'

He nodded and made no comment at that, then said, 'So, where is your Mr Loader? have you seen him recently?'

'No I'm afraid not, but he came to my house about two weeks ago.' I used the word house deliberately because I didn't want him to know I was now a farmer from Tasmania.

'Well, young man, he came to see me a few days ago, saying that he would return soon. But so far he hasn't.'

'So he is in Britain, then?' I answered. He nodded in the affirmative. 'Do you have any idea where he might be?' I said. 'Not a clue,' he said, as he shook his head slowly.

I blinked in surprise at the Professor and my jaw opened slightly. Fiona was looking at me askance and obviously puzzled too. This meant that Loader was certainly somewhere in Britain, but where?

The Professor walked around his desk, opened a drawer, taking out a letter similar to mine, opened it, and put the two slips of paper together. They fitted together having been creased and then torn apart. In some curious way this seemed to satisfy him.

'Please sit down and make your selves comfortable,' he said, as he pressed a button on the desk. 'I have a special historical book about the Bodleian Library which will, I hope, be of immense help to you.'

He passed a book to me with great care and I studied it briefly with interest, because it was partly about Bishop Tanner's life and times and his magnificent gifts to the Bodleian Library.

While we waited, he gave us a brief outline of what he knew about Bishop Thomas Tanner. Then he took me along to his small room, as he called it, leaving Fiona alone. He explained that it was a small room and not big enough for three people. It was an air-conditioned safe room, with a time lock and a coded key.

'Now I have you alone,' he said rather seriously, 'what do you know about your companion? You obviously have security clearance, but what about her? She is a journalist, which makes me a trifle nervous!'

The question stumped me for a moment, so I just simply said, 'She is an architectural photographic journalist. Not an ordinary journalist in the way that you perhaps mean.'

'How can you be sure that she is reliable and security safe? You realise this is a very important part of the forthcoming agreement between the Irish and British Governments.'

'You know about the agreement then?'

'Yes, I was interviewed by Special Branch and it wasn't very pleasant. They wanted to know about my history – and too much about my personal life.'

'But I understand you are a man of distinction, surely you wouldn't have any problems?'

'That's what I thought, but I have been married twice and that's what they questioned me closely about. It was damned embarrassing.'

'Cheeky blighters,' I said, 'but that doesn't help you with the problem of Fiona. I am willing to stake my life on her honesty and integrity.'

He seemed satisfied with my answer and then followed with the remark, 'That's now your full responsibility. You also realise, that apart from Loader, the Special Branch are chasing after you too.'

'Heck, why are they chasing me?' I said slightly mystified.

'Because time is running out and the agreement is getting close,' he said. 'Now let's get down to the facts. When the Bishop left his mass of papers to us at the Bodleian Library, the bulk of them came from the Cathedral at Norwich, a little came from St Asaph in North Wales, and some from the village in Wiltshire where Bishop Tanner was born.

'Did you know that the barge transporting the bulk of the collection from Norwich to Oxford sank in December 1731, and some of the books and manuscripts were damaged? The bulk of it was saved however, near the town of Wallingford about 10 miles from Oxford. There is a river lock and weir.'

He continued, showing me an old map. 'Perhaps that is where the accident occurred.' He pointed to a spot on the old map.

I studied the old map and could see the possible problem with navigating a long barge past a lock and weir, around an island in the middle of the River Thames. The water would have been freezing in December, making it not easy to rescue valuable items in such conditions. Then he continued.

'I have cross-checked the list supplied from Norwich and St Asaph, and they are all there. Also, he apparently had a considerable collection of coins and medals, some of which were stolen in 1732, which brings us to the question – were the manuscript pages taken at the same time?'

'No, it's not likely, because of course we have a photograph of at least one of the missing pages. They were photographed by someone in Wiltshire, before the Second World War.'

'Ah! Of course, that's true. I had forgotten,' he replied, sadly remembering his old friend and colleague who had started this whole quest and was killed for his efforts. 'So where do we go from here?'

'Everything is pointing to this village in Wiltshire,' I said. 'Although it's difficult to believe. I have been there already and found nothing'.

'This is most disappointing,' he replied. 'I've just remembered something else too. The Irish Special Branch is also now involved in this chase as well – did you know?'

I didn't say anything to this surprising news, but just thought, 'Oh no!' and nodded understandingly. This whole thing had suddenly become top heavy, but it did reflect the seriousness of the situation. I had always regarded this quest as my own and was not happy with this new development. We stood looking at one another, not knowing what to say. I was the first one to break the silence.

'This is getting us nowhere, Professor. I will return later if I find anything of help, but it seems the only clue is to return to Wiltshire.' I shook my head in disbelief.

'Well, good luck,' was his quiet reply. We shook hands warmly, wished each other well, and parted.

Fiona and I returned to Bristol the way we had come, not saying very much, then she suddenly said, 'What was going on in the little room? That was rather strange!' There was disappointment in her voice.

'Yes, it was strange. I'm sorry – it was rather rude of me. I should have explained, but it was all about you, I'm afraid,' I replied softly.

'Me! Whatever do you mean?' she said.

'Have you ever been checked by Special Branch?'

'No, of course not. Well, not to my knowledge. No! Why would they check on me?'

'Well, the Professor has been. And they asked him some awkward questions which he didn't like. You see, his first wife died and eventually he re-married.'

'What sort of questions?' she said.

'He was married, but this time to an Irish Roman Catholic lady whom he met at Trinity College Dublin when he was researching the *Book of Kells*. Innocent enough, you would think! They became good friends and eventually married.'

Fiona laughed and said, 'I can understand that, they have to be so precise and careful. Surely you can understand their reasoning?'

'Yes, I suppose so, but he took offence at the questioning of his private life, which he thought was none of their business. So the officer who interviewed him warned him not to discuss the matter with anyone, especially his wife, and he took this rather personally.'

We continued our journey back to Bristol, partly to return Harry's car and partly because we couldn't think where else to look. Our route took us through North Wiltshire and we were tempted to go to Devizes and start again, as it was where I had begun my original quest. I was not happy with the way things were going, especially the intervention of Special Branch. I felt it was a criticism of my own ability to bring this quest to a successful conclusion.

Fiona interrupted my troubled thoughts, by saying, 'Why don't we have a relaxing meal in Bristol city centre? There are several good places to eat.'

'Sounds great,' I said. 'I'm very much in need of a quiet moment to mull things over. Let's go.'

'I've got an even better idea,' she said. 'We'll go to Bath instead – it's closer. And there's a charming hotel, too, with a five star rating restaurant, with a superb chef.'

We stopped by the side of the road and swapped drivers so that Fiona could drive into Bath, because she knew the route. We parked in a dignified

Georgian square and went into the hotel restaurant which exuded expensive elegance and old charm. Fiona whispered, 'This is my treat, remember!'

'Glad to hear it. Thank you,' I replied solemnly, as the waiter led us to a table in the centre of the room. The table next to ours was occupied by a young, good looking couple holding hands across the table. They did look up at us briefly as we passed their table. They smiled fleetingly and carried on chatting.

We engaged in light conversation about the weather and nothing in particular, to allay any suspicions. The meal came and Fiona was right about the chef. I had Beef Wellington for my main course and enjoyed it very much. Fiona had Royal Salmon, her favourite dish, and we finished with an elaborate ice cream each.

It was while we were finishing our coffee, that the young Scottish couple introduced themselves. I had seen them earlier, casting curious glances at us, rather in the manner that normal ordinary people do, when they see a celebrity in the street or hotel. This puzzled and concerned me, but I didn't mention it to Fiona. Then the young man leant across and whispered, 'You're Jack Harrison aren't you?'

This was bad news for me, so I replied equally quietly, 'What makes you say that?'

'They found your car in mid-Wales and the police are searching for you. It's in the national papers today. Here, I'll show you your photograph.'

As he reached for the newspaper beside him, I put my hand on his forearm to prevent him showing the article. 'Don't show it, please,' I whispered, 'the situation is even more complex than you can imagine. My boss will be furious,' meaning Loader.

It was probably Loader's frantic attempt to flush me out into the open. I was not pleased with the latest development, especially with Special Branch muscling in and the villains closing around me. On top of this worrying turn of events, I still hadn't found the missing pages. Fiona had been quietly watching the action and listening to the conversation. She motioned that we should get moving. She paid the bill as promised and I thanked her with a hug. Then we turned in the direction of the door, smiling at the young couple as we made our way out.

We both felt happy and relaxed, but as we turned on to the footpath to return to our car, we were confronted by the three people we didn't want to see. The one with the smashed nose stepped forward aggressively, and muttered through his clenched teeth, 'Where are the manuscripts? We want them now!'

'I'm sorry, you ugly bastard. I haven't got them – and that's the truth. You didn't bring your guns this time, I notice?' I said sarcastically.

'You're lying, Harrison!' he screamed, and went for my throat, his hands tightening around my neck and squeezing very hard.

I stood still for just a split second and then calmly brought my two hands together in front of me and drove upwards fiercely in one swift movement and came down viciously on his nose. It was the stupidest movement he could have made, because his nose was still in bad shape. He staggered back, screaming in pain, bleeding, and fell down. Just for good measure, I stamped hard on his foot.

As I did so, Fiona unexpectedly stepped forward and kicked the other man in the knee and followed this by scraping down his shin with the heel of her shoe. The third man moved forward to attack, but then thought better of it. He just stood there with his mouth open. He realised that he was now out-numbered, then attempted to help the other two to their feet. They all limped off together.

A soft voice beside me said quietly, 'That was very impressive, I must say,' with a Scottish accent. I turned slightly and he continued. 'Yes, we are on holiday here in Bath. It's been a rather eventful day and I thought I should help you if necessary.'

'Thanks for the kind thought,' I replied with a grin. 'Your very presence was probably the final blow to them. They probably thought you were coming to our aid.'

'Yes,' he said calmly, 'I would've, but you seemed to have the situation well under control.'

I sized him up quickly. He was well built and rugged looking. I reckoned he could give a good account of himself, if called upon in a fight. The big surprise, however, was Fiona, who was grinning slightly beside me. I gave her a hug and whispered in her ear, 'Well done! But I think we had better move from here quickly, just in case someone saw the action and calls the police – I don't want that.'

She nodded in understanding. We swiftly shook hands with the young couple, thanked them and were on our way.

To get back to Bristol quickly, we were bound to travel through the old Roman city of Bath. I was driving while Fiona directed me and kept an eye out for our pursuers.

'Do you remember when we were changing drivers on our way here into Bath? Perhaps that's when they saw us and followed,' I reasoned.

Fiona nodded in agreement and I drove on uneventfully to Bristol and through the city to the famous Clifton area. It wasn't until we reached the Clifton Suspension Bridge that things started to go wrong again.

We had just got onto Brunel's famous old bridge, when the traffic stopped for no apparent reason. Eventually people were getting out of their cars and showing a certain amount of irritation, and then as seconds went by, some drivers were starting to get very angry.

Feeling confident that the blockage would soon clear, I didn't get out of the car, but when I did, it was obvious that the blockage was caused by the thugs who had attacked us outside the restaurant. Up ahead of us, one of the big limousines had stopped and two thugs were looking into the engine bay, pretending that they had broken down. I turned around and looked behind me, and to my surprise three more of them, including the one with the sore red nose, started walking towards us across the bridge.

Fiona got out of the car also and shouted a warning to me. 'Get in Jack!'

I felt as if I was about to do battle again, which was eminently possible, because we were now trapped on the old Suspension Bridge, very high up in the middle of the Avon River gorge. Suddenly, the blockage cleared and changed for the better, two burly figures got out of another car between us and the thugs behind, and started to talk to them and forcefully directed them to return to their limousine. That takes care of them I thought. Then, as if by magic, a tow truck appeared at the far end ahead of us. In spite of their loud angry protests, they were towed away.

The column of cars moved off, including us, but the two burly figures behind us – who were either police or Special Branch – held them up long enough for us to return safely to Fiona's apartment. We were greeted with joy and relief by Kate and Alan, especially Alan who was very pleased to get his own car back in one piece, although he had enjoyed his drive in Fiona's car. I wisely didn't tell him about the Austin 1800 debacle in mid-Wales.

Kate and Alan were excellent company, and listened to our account of the day with interest, while sitting around the dining table and afterwards we talked about the City of Bristol and its long history. We couldn't seem to get Alan and Kate away from the subject of the *Book of Kells* and my interest in calligraphy. They couldn't see the link between the book and my farm in Tasmania, but I didn't want to tell them the real connection. To get them off the subject, Fiona looked up Tasmania on the computer, which the three of them thoroughly enjoyed. It saved the difficult situation for me.

We all retired to bed early, but Fiona and I had some serious thinking to do, so we discussed our plans for the next day. Both cars were now locked away out of sight and safe from prying eyes, so we slept soundly.

BACK TO WILTSHIRE

The following morning, having made our plans the previous evening, we took Fiona's MG out of its hiding place and speedily drove south into Somerset for approximately half an hour, then turned east into Wiltshire, and finally turned north through the middle of Salisbury Plain.

The purpose of our circuitous route was to shake off any possible pursuers which, as it turned out, we didn't have, but it was wise to do so, because they had two cars cruising round the countryside looking for us, almost certainly with a phone in each car.

Eventually we arrived at Market Lavington without any problems, drew up at the Vicarage, and before we could knock at the front door, it opened and the Reverend was there with an enormous smile on his face.

'Good news,' he stated emphatically. 'Come inside and have a cuppa and I'll tell you what I have discovered.'

I had been in this position before and had been disappointed so often, but it did sound more promising. However, I didn't get too excited. Fiona, on the other hand, was very hopeful.

'Let me introduce Fiona,' I said, 'a colleague and fellow companion, who has been of tremendous help.'

'Not your girlfriend, then?' he replied with a grin.

'Well, we only just met last week on my way to St Asaph Cathedral.'

'Did you have any luck at St Asaph Cathedral?' he queried.

'Well, yes and no. According to the Dean there, everything now seems to point to this village.'

'That's strangely interesting,' he replied, 'because you see, what I didn't know when you were here last, was that after the Second World War – and I'm still unsure which year – the Vicarage changed and came to this house. Prior to this it was in a much larger house with extensive grounds. It is still there now – but as a nursing home. I have permission to visit it today, so your timing is perfect,' he said with a satisfied smile. I sincerely hoped with all my heart that he was right.

After our morning tea break, with the Reverend and his wife Carolyn, who as usual seemed as enthusiastic as we did, we walked through the village up to the nursing home.

We were formally introduced to the Matron Grandville, who was curious and delighted to be of help. She whispered that we were welcome to search for any documents that would help us.

We started in the roof space, and worked our way meticulously down through the big house. We did everything possible, tapping walls for false panels or old cupboards that might have been plastered over. The Matron, who had known the building before the most recent renovations, became very enthusiastic and helpful and allowed us to look under carpets and move furniture, because it made her feel important, which of course she was. We couldn't have done it without her permission.

Finally, we reached the basement and searched thoroughly, although it was dark and dingy. Fiona wasn't keen on the spiders and pleaded to go out into the fresh air. The Reverend and I continued our search, but it was all to no avail. Disappointment was written all over our faces, especially the Matron's; although not fully understanding our quest, she apologised sincerely. We returned to the Vicarage having exhausted ourselves, chatting as we went back, about every thing except of course the *Book of Kells* and the missing pages.

Fiona and I tried to cheer us all up, but just couldn't raise a smile from anyone. If anyone could brighten up our gloomy mood it would be Fiona, but in spite of her valiant efforts, nothing seemed to work – we were all totally exhausted.

We were sitting down having afternoon tea in the front room when the Reverend got to his feet as if there was something he had forgotten.

'Goodness! I've just remembered something rather important. We've searched in both Vicarages now and found nothing, right? So what if we've been searching in the wrong house? Do we know which house was the Vicarage when the Bishop and his father lived here?' There was silence because no-one was sure.

'We have an excellent little museum in the village,' he continued. 'Surely they would know the answer to my question, wouldn't they?'

We agreed with this idea immediately. It broke the sombre mood and we went quickly to the museum. The part-time volunteer curator had just opened up and was delighted to suddenly have so many customers. The Reverend put the all important question to him and the answer came back immediately.

'Well, Reverend, I've always believed that Bishop Tanner was in the Vicarage house that you are in now. It's much older than what is the nursing home, you know.'

'Of course I should have known of that myself,' said the Reverend.

There was an unexpected silence while the news sank in. The curator could see we were surprised and disappointed, and then he quickly said,

'But I can double check with all our records and the County Archivist at Trowbridge. Or perhaps with the old museum at Devizes. However, they would be more inclined to archaeological records: Stonehenge, Avebury, the many tumuli and round barrows and long barrows and all that pre- history stuff.'

This was the second setback of the day so we sadly returned to the Vicarage. I felt that as they had all been so co-operative and helpful, I owed them a brief explanation of the overall reasons for my search, and the upcoming talks between the Irish and British Governments. I told them of the tremendous pressure on me, but pleaded with them to keep the information to themselves. They solemnly promised they would and I felt very confident that they would keep their word.

The Reverend and his good lady persuaded us to the stay the night, which we accepted very gladly, as this would be so convenient. As we were about to retire at 10 o'clock there was a quiet knock at the front door.

'One of my parishioners, I expect,' said the Reverend. 'It might be a problem with a sick person.'

So we left him to deal with the visitor. There was a quiet conversation in the hallway which I couldn't hear, although it sounded very much like the Matron from the nursing home. It was more of a pastoral care problem, I assumed. So the rest of us went to bed and slept soundly.

ANOTHER CLUE

Next morning, the bright sunshine was streaming into my bedroom and woke me. I turned over, got up and went to the bathroom. I remembered that I had no wash bag for an overnight stay, but I washed thoroughly and went unshaven down to breakfast. I was the last to arrive for the meal.

There was a quiet group sitting at the table in the big bright kitchen and again I couldn't think of our next move, if indeed there was one, apart from a house to house search of the whole village, which would be impossible and unpopular. However Paul seemed to be in a positive mood for some reason – perhaps it had something to do with last night's visitor – but he was keeping quiet for the moment. As soon as the breakfast was cleared away and the table was free, he sat us down and started to speak.

'As you know I had a visitor last night. It was the Matron Grandville. She gave me a clue as to some possible information about the missing pages of the *Book of Kells*, but I do have some further enquiries to make before I can be totally sure.'

I sat bolt upright. At last this was what I wanted to hear. 'What enquiries are those? Please – tell us more,' I said with unrestrained eagerness.

He shook his head adamantly and wouldn't say any more, except to ask us to come back late on Friday afternoon for a meal and to park Fiona's car in the small drive at the side of the Vicarage. This all sounded very mysterious, but he wouldn't be drawn on the subject any further.

'Do you mean this Friday?' I said politely. 'That seems odd!'

The expression in Fiona's deep brown eyes however was a joy to see. She was probably thinking of a new article she would write to accompany her photographs of the pages, and about our adventure, but much later. It would be a well deserved triumph for her certainly, and she had earned it after the enthusiastic support she had given me.

'It will become clear on Friday night,' Paul replied calmly. 'I can't say any more, but I hope it will be successful.'

As we drove back to Bristol, deep in thought, Fiona suddenly said, 'Why the mystery about Friday night I wonder? I can hardly wait.'

'I don't get it either, unless he doesn't want to disappoint us with another false trail.'

'Yes that could be the only thing that makes sense. He may not be too confident of his information.'

'We've drawn a blank almost everywhere else,' I said thoughtfully.

'Right. I'm going to take you to Dorset. To Lyme Regis, for a well earned break. Get your mind off this business – the seaside air will do you good.'

'I like the sound of that,' I replied. Once again, Fiona had come up with a bright idea. I was getting obsessed with chasing these damned elusive pages. If I failed, I could tell Loader that I had at least tried really hard and given it my best effort, despite whatever doubts others in the Department might have – now that I was no longer really one of them.

We drove quickly south into the County of Dorset and stayed at an old hotel in Wareham, and then went on to Lyme Regis to look for dinosaur bones from a recent cliff fall that Fiona had read about in the newspapers. We walked along the famous Cob Harbour holding hands like a pair of young lovers. Finally we had a brief look at Chesil Beach and then returned to our hotel.

We slept well and felt refreshed with high hopes for our journey back to Market Lavington on Friday. However, we had to travel to Fiona's apartment first, to borrow some old gardening clothes for me, from Alan. This was at the suggestion of Paul, who had phoned to say they would be needed. It was an interesting twist, giving the strong impression that we would be digging perhaps for something somewhere. I was wishing that I had a better understanding of what Paul was up to, but still could not extract any further information from him.

I thought of all the interesting places I had visited in my quest and now there was a faint chance it was coming to a successful conclusion. Of course, I had met Fiona, which was something very pleasant to think seriously about. I then tried to concentrate on the missing pages, which after all was the main reason I was being paid a lot of money. If I failed, would it make any difference to the upcoming accord between the British and Irish Governments? I couldn't be sure, but it would bring favourable publicity to the talks. It would smooth the path of progress and my Father and Mother would be happy for me. I planned to ring them afterwards if we were successful; but if not, I wouldn't mention it.

We arrived at the Vicarage late in the afternoon, which by then was very hot and humid.

We followed Paul's instructions and parked Fiona's car in the side drive. Paul's weather-beaten old Land Rover was curiously, I thought, left outside in the road facing down the slope. After a warm greeting from our hosts, we all went to bed early at Paul's insistence. He still told us nothing, but promised he would explain fully to me in the morning.

Eventually I dozed off, but slept fitfully because of everything churning over in my mind. Paul's insistence on being so secretive was strange, and questions in my mind about Fiona also played a large part in these many thoughts.

A STORMY NIGHT

I was gently awakened by Paul who put his hand over my mouth and whispered, 'Sshhh! Get dressed quickly – in your old gardening clothes.'

I looked at the bedside clock – it was 2a.m. I dressed silently and joined him at the front door. He stood there with his finger up to his lips, opened the door slowly, ushered me out and closing the door quietly, got into the old Land Rover. He whispered to me to push the vehicle, because he didn't want to start the engine. As soon as it was rolling down the slope, I got in, but didn't slam the door, just pulled it to with a click.

When we reached the old mill and the river, which was the lowest point between the two villages, he started the engine and continued slowly in second gear, keeping the revs down and the engine noise low.

The old Land Rover engine growled its way through West Lavington, and then started to rise slowly up the slope towards the edge of Salisbury Plain. It was at this point that my curiosity became so overwhelming that I could not keep silent any longer. I asked him where we were going, and why.

'Imber,' he said quite simply, but didn't elaborate.

'What's Imber?' I said.

'It's the deserted ghost village on the northern edge of Salisbury Plain.'

I still didn't comprehend. 'Why's it deserted?' I asked with increasing interest.

'During the Second World War the villagers were evacuated from the village by the War Office – now the Ministry of Defence. The villagers believed they were doing their part for the war effort. They thought and imagined they would be going back again, after it was all over. The American Army was – so the story goes – allowed to do training for house to house fighting prior to the D-Day invasion on the 6 June 1944. At least that's what they were told.'

'Do you mean after all this time they haven't been allowed back?'

'No. Except on special occasions, like funerals or celebrations. But many restrictions apply – and only with the permission of the MOD.'

I said nothing, but absorbed this information, until he broke the silence again. 'Now this is called St Joan á Gore's Cross,' he announced as we slowed down, looking for a way forward into the field.

There was a barrier across the track. We eventually found a partial route where the ditch had filled in and we crept forward slowly and silently, passing a sign saying 'NO ENTRY'.

The weather, which had been so brilliant most of the time since my return to England, decided to become unpleasant and began to rain, gently at first, and then the wind started to blow. Soon it turned into a full-scale storm, the rain lashing almost horizontally as we sat in the vehicle in silence.

Paul was thinking what to do next. I was of no help, because his full plan was still not clear, and I was wondering where he was leading me. All I knew was that this was MOD property. We couldn't put the lights on to see our way forward, and there was no road – it was just a muddy track churned over by tanks and army trucks. He obviously knew this area well, because he kept referring to an old 1930 map which he had strapped to his knee.

'I took special notice of the weather forecast,' he said. 'But it didn't promise to be this awful. This storm must be a sudden cold front coming in from the North Sea.'

Paul had stopped the Land Rover, hoping that the storm would die down, but all that happened was one fierce gust ripped off the wiper on my side of the windscreen. He turned the vehicle slightly in an attempt to keep our vision clear. Suddenly there was a flash of lightning and a tremendous clap of thunder. We were obviously very close to the centre of the storm.

There was another flash and Paul said, 'Thank you Lord – did you see that Jack?'

'No, what was it?' I said, surprised by his sudden enthusiasm.

'The Church, Jack, the Church! It's St Giles' Church! We are looking straight at it. He engaged first gear and slowly drove up the slope to the Church. 'This Church dates from the 13th and 14th centuries,' he said. 'And it's believed to have been built on an even earlier Norman Church.'

I could hardly concentrate on what Paul was saying, so intense was my excitement and the violence of the storm.

We waited for another flash of lightning to get a better view. Paul drove around the Church which was surrounded by a high, barbed wire fence. He said he was looking for an opening where we could enter the Church.

'That's what I'm looking for,' he emphasised, pointing at a hole in the building. 'There is a shell hole in the chancel wall. Can you see it? Look there!' his voice was rising as he spoke.

We got through the barbed wire fence and walked cautiously across the sodden grass. Paul had brought a canvas bag with some tools of various descriptions. He took out a torch and switched it on, holding it downwards to confirm that it was the shell hole. The army had put a rusty piece of corrugated iron over it, and two timber stakes which were now rotting.

We moved the iron sheet and Paul, being the slightly smaller of the two of us, wriggled in with great difficulty and whispered: 'Pass the canvas bag. Stay outside and keep guard.'

I had no idea what he was attempting to do in there, except searching. He obviously knew where to look. I sheltered in the lee side of a church buttress and tried to keep warm by walking on the spot, stamping my feet and moving my arms about.

I estimated he had been in there about five or ten minutes when his muffled voice called softly: 'I need your help Jack. Can you get through the hole?'

His voice had an urgent tone to it, so I struggled through the gap and fell the last bit onto the dust covered floor. I switched on my torch and Paul said quickly, 'Keep it pointing downwards! We don't want anyone to see a light.'

In my excitement I forgot. 'Sorry!' I whispered back.

'We are not supposed to be here in Imber, because it is still a Ministry of Defence site. If they catch us I'm in very serious trouble with the Church as well as the British Army. If you can work your way over to me, we can do this together. See this tomb?' he said, pointing out a path along the dusty floor with his torch.

I raised my torch slightly and followed his beam over towards a white marble tomb with a ghostly figure of a knight lying on a raised platform. I jumped back slightly, very surprised. It was a medieval knight with chain mail coat, a helmet with raised visor, and a sword. At his feet was a small crouching lion.

'They are the tombs of the Rous Family. Crusaders from medieval times,' he said. 'And there is the other one,' he said, moving his torch again slowly across the floor. This was a completely different design. It had a shield blazoned with three rampant lions. Two battered angels supported the head of the knight, and there was a huge lion at his feet.

'I am surprised. I would have imagined that there was nothing left here after all this time' I said in a whisper.

'Yes, indeed, you're right,' Paul replied softly. 'Now come and give me a hand. As I lever this panel off the end of the platform of the first tomb, please try and catch it as it falls.'

I followed his instructions to the letter. As he worked away at the last joint, the panel fell down suddenly into the dust and although I caught it briefly, it was so heavy that it fell with a thud. There was a sharp intake of breath from Paul, but we realised the marble slab was fortunately still intact.

'That was lucky. Now let's have a look inside. Please bring your torch.' He produced a small brush from the canvas bag and carefully swept out the space. 'There it is! There it is!' he said, with mounting excitement.

I couldn't see much until he carefully brought it out. It was a dark wooden box with brass fittings and corners. It looked like an old portable writing desk, the kind that was much prized by Victorians and modern day antique dealers.

'It's locked of course,' he muttered. 'Naturally, the key would be in the possession of the person or persons who put it here.'

'Do we know who they were?' I asked.

'Well, yes and no. I know the family. But they have sworn me to absolute secrecy and I must respect their trust in me.'

He brushed the box again so I could see it better.

'The box on its own would be worth a fair bit on the antique market but it's the contents that interest me,' I whispered.

I held onto the box with one hand and the torch with the other, so that Paul could pack the tools in his canvas bag. He then wriggled through the shell hole first. I passed the bag out to him, and then the box which we had wrapped in an old sack cloth for its protection. Paul placed our find carefully in the back of the vehicle behind his seat and we both climbed in to head for home.

The rain had slowed slightly as we eased our way gingerly with the Land Rover through the wet, slippery grass. It would be dawn in about two hours, so we drove cautiously down the slope.

When we reached what I assumed was originally the main street of the now silent and ruined village, we passed another Ministry of Defence sign warning us of possible unexploded ammunition, and to keep to the main road. That didn't settle my nerves much – I couldn't see any road.

Paul suddenly stopped driving and through the rainy mist I could see five shadowy figures with guns approaching us. Behind them was a Saracen six-wheeled armoured personnel carrier. 'We are in serious trouble now,' Paul muttered.

'What do we do?' I whispered back.

The question was answered by the nearest figure who moved aggressively towards us, shining his powerful torch in our faces.

'Right – you two! Out of the vehicle!' he ordered. 'Keep them covered!' he shouted a command to the others. 'Now what the blazes are you doing in a restricted military area? Do you realise you could get blown to hell?'

'I don't think so, Captain,' replied Paul. 'We have the Lord on our side.'

There was a muffled chuckle from the men behind the Captain, which he didn't appreciate at all.

'Alright you lot – shut it. I'm not in a very good mood. You're in enough trouble as it is because of your damned incompetence,' he shouted.

Paul then moved forward to calm the situation and started to speak. 'May I show you what we have, and why we are here? Then perhaps you will understand?'

My heart stopped pumping and my brain went into a spin. Surely, after all this trouble, he wasn't going to show the box to these army people.

'I should explain that I am Paul Charlton, Vicar of St Mary's, Market Lavington.'

'Have you any proof of this claim?' was the terse reply.

Paul pulled his waterproof cape away from his neck to show his dog collar.

'That doesn't prove a damned thing, does it?' he said. 'I'm going to have to check your vehicle thoroughly. I'm Captain Stewart, and I'm in charge here,' he continued, loudly emphasising the words 'in charge'.

Captain Stewart and Paul then strode over to the Land Rover and sat in the front seats for several minutes while the rest of us stood in the drizzling conditions. Although the storm had passed over, it was still cold, wet and miserable standing there, and I couldn't hear what was being said.

Eventually they came out and to my total surprise shook hands cordially and the Captain said, less sternly this time, 'Please do not enter my territory again without my permission. This is an extremely dangerous area with live ammunition everywhere.'

Totally puzzled, I got back in the Land Rover with Paul and we drove behind the Army Saracen, with our side lights on, towards the barrier. One of the soldiers opened the barrier and let us out.

My curiosity knew no bounds. I was bursting with questions. Paul sensed my impatience and then finally clarified the whole of the last ten minutes.

'I showed him the photos I had taken on my digital camera of the frescos on the north wall of the nave. And the incredible marble tombs. I told him absolutely everything I knew about the history of the Church, which was quite a lot,' he added.

'Yes, but what about the old oak box?' I asked impatiently.

'Well, if you remember, it was behind my seat on the floor. I covered it with the picnic blanket, but told him it was a dog's blanket covered in dog fur, so he didn't bother to look under it.'

I chuckled with laughter, 'But you haven't got a dog, have you?'

'We did once. Dear old Rex finally came in handy.'

'But what about those frescos you were talking about? I didn't see any frescos or murals.'

'Well, they are there, but sadly very faded. They were painted in the 17th century we believe,' he said.

'This Church is so full of surprises. It's complete with astonishing treasures. What a sad end to such a long and honourable history,' I said with un-muted anger.

'I couldn't express it better,' he replied sombrely.

'What made Captain Stewart change his aggressive attitude so quickly?' I said, full of curiosity.

'I told him also I was not impressed with the shell hole in the chancel and the botched repair, which I said was disgraceful. I put him on the back foot immediately, so things improved from there.'

'Many, many thanks Paul. This is so important for my quest. You negotiated well.'

St. Mary's Church, Market Lavington.

'Don't thank me. I did it for the missing pages, but also for the poor old Church. However, I did promise to stick to the rules in future,' he muttered regretfully.

'Well, that's fair enough. But we now have the oak box.'

'Yes, but we haven't checked the contents yet,' he said.

'That's true, but I feel fairly positive that we may have the long lost pages at last.'

'So do I,' he said, 'so do I. I can see you are as keen as I to unlock the box and look inside. Let's go back to St Mary's Church and open the box, although we haven't got the key.'

'Don't worry,' I said. 'My skills at lock-picking are excellent. It shouldn't prove too difficult.' This was one of the many skills I learned during my extensive training in London.

We parked the Land Rover and slowly walked up the cobbled path to the main entrance of St Mary's Church. Because of the wet conditions, it was still moist and slippery although the storm had finally finished. Paul was carrying the box. He stumbled, but I managed to catch him before he fell heavily to the ground – my heart skipped a beat. It was a tense moment because of our very precious cargo.

We stopped in front of the porch and he handed me the box while he searched for the key. We went in the outer door, laid the box down on the old seat in the porch for a moment, while we took off our heavy waterproof coats because they were extremely wet, and then made our way silently into the Church. Paul led the way in the dim light – we didn't want to put the main lights on. We reached the vestry safely, switched on the small desk lamp and placed the box down securely on the desk so I could pick the lock.

It was a very old box with the date '1668' picked out rather crudely with a nail and hammer, in a series of dots. It was obviously by an amateur craftsman, with someone's initials below. These initials were badly worn away clearly by constant use, probably as an everyday object and one now of great age.

'It's a 17th century English oak deed box,' Paul said confidently. 'Right, over to you. Are you sure you can unlock it?'

I looked at the box again and brushed more dust and dirt off to examine it thoroughly.

'If you can't pick the lock we might have to break it open,' Paul said.

'I'd rather not,' I said, 'because of its age and history. I wonder how much it's worth as an antique?'

'Because of its age and rarity, I would think it would be worth about four or five hundred pounds. It's only a rough, wild guess. I'm not an antique expert.'

The box had a lock on the front and didn't look too difficult, so I put my lock-picker's kit down on the desk and started to work on the tumblers, with occasional blobs of oil. However, they gave me a lot of trouble because of the dirt in the lock and the age of it. Paul said that he had been told that it had not been used since the middle of the Second World War.

Finally the lock gave way with a satisfying click. The moment of truth had arrived as we looked at one another with apprehension and excitement.

'You go first,' Paul said. 'This is your quest.'

'Thank you,' I whispered.

I cautiously lifted the lid to reveal a leather pouch and silk cloth which I removed carefully and unwrapped, revealing another fabric which seemed to be linen or cotton. I lifted this up and laid it flat on the table. I held my breath and folded back the last flap to discover a magnificent work of art. We remained totally silent, admiring the incredible workmanship, with colours almost as vibrant as the day they had been finished.

'This must be it,' Paul murmured. 'But the pages seem slightly bigger than the ones in Trinity College, Dublin.'

'I hope you are not saying that these aren't the missing pages after all?'

'Not at all. Somewhere in its long history it was rebound several times, and the pages were trimmed in pre-Victorian times. But not these. If you look carefully, you can see the uneven edges. The pages I saw in Dublin were the ones that had been trimmed straight, much later in time,' he said.

'You're quite right, of course,' I said. 'Loader also mentioned something about that to me.'

We laid the first page to one side and un-wrapped the next page, which was equally stunning. We looked at yet another page and I now felt so strongly that we had found the missing pages, but as I turned to comment to Paul, a voice spoke from the darkness of the doorway. Paul was looking open-mouthed past me, towards the door.

'Thank you, Harrison. I warned you we would meet again!' Mazuchelli announced in triumph.

'Damn it, in our excitement we forgot to lock the porch door,' I muttered to Paul.

Paul didn't speak. He just stared at me in total silence.

'Leave the box and step back from the desk. Now!' ordered Mazuchelli.

I recognised his unpleasant voice from Amsterdam and realised we had been ambushed. Paul also sensed we were in serious trouble. We reluctantly did as Mazuchelli demanded because there were two other men behind him holding pistols. They stepped forward pointing them aggressively.

We were then brutally marched by the two gunmen, through the Church towards the bell tower. Mazuchelli stayed in the vestry with the box and the missing pages.

'Open the door, now,' said the angry voice behind me, as we reached the bell tower door.

'Say please, if you don't mind – any way, I don't have the key,' I answered, only to receive a vicious kick in the back of the knee. Paul half turned to speak.

'I must protest. This is the house of God, you Philistines.' For his courage he got the same treatment.

'Now open the door!' said the voice, shouting loudly.

Paul fumbled in his coat pocket for the key and searched for the keyhole of the very solid oak door. We were prodded and cajoled slowly up the stone staircase, which was well worn by centuries of bellringers, and the many men who tended to the clock.

As we ascended, Paul got slightly faster and I followed in his footsteps, but I thought he was acting strangely. He was quietly counting: three, two, one, ten, and again as we reached higher. I was beginning to understand what he was trying to tell me as we reached the half landing, because they were obviously intending to shoot us dead at any moment.

We were slightly ahead of them because we were fitter, when Paul repeated his counting and we turned together and struck them hard, taking them by the right hand and wrist, hitting them in the face.

One of the pistols went off in the struggle, the bullet striking the treble bell in the tower. The bells had, of course, been in the up resting position which is their normal place. Another bullet zinged its way into the upper part of the tower. The first bullet had dislodged the bell from its position and it rang once very loudly.

The surprise of this caused my opponent to pause long enough for me to give him a vicious right hand punch to the jaw, which sent him sprawling across the dusty balcony and over the wooden rail. He landed on the platform below.

The six bell ropes went from the bells down through this platform to where the bellringers would stand below. He ended up with his leg stuck through the flimsy platform and hanging on to the bell rope, crying out in Italian for help. In his fall over the rail, he had dropped his pistol on the floor, which I picked up immediately and turned round to help Paul but he didn't need much help, having pinned his assailant to the old timber floor.

I leaned down and put the pistol to the thug's throat. He gave in without a struggle and looked terrified, pleading for mercy. I had to admit I did not like firearms, so putting him to sleep permanently was not an option for me. I passed the pistol to Paul and pulled the man roughly to his feet, then thumped him as hard as possible in the stomach. As he doubled up, I gave him a left hook to the jaw which settled the matter.

We tied this one up firmly for good measure and left him face down in the dust. We made our way silently down the stairs to the bottom and locked the solid oak door quietly to keep the two of them jailed for the time being.

Out of the dim light came Loader's voice as we walked carefully down the central aisle towards the altar, which was the widest part of the Church, for safety.

'That you, Jack?' he asked nervously.

'Yes, where are you?' I could tell something was wrong by the uncertainty in his voice.

'Where's Mazuchelli?' I said.

'Right behind Loader. With a loaded gun,' said Mazuchelli, who appeared from behind the square stone column. He showed me his gun, arming it with a load click in the dim light. It was a stand-off. I approached the two of them cautiously. Paul meanwhile was moving silently round to the back of them, keeping down low, in between the pews.

In a moment the situation changed dramatically. The door opened and Fiona and Paul's wife Carolyn came in, amiably chatting away and put the lights on without realising the great danger. This caused Mazuchelli to drop his guard slightly, and I took this opportunity by pushing Loader sideways with my right forearm and moving quickly at Mazuchelli's gun.

Moving upwards with my left hand I smashed my right fist into his surprised and unpleasant face. He staggered backwards hard against the wall just as Paul grabbed his other hand. He tried to reply by throwing a wild punch at my head, but missed. I disarmed him quickly and emptied the pistol, putting the bullets in my pocket. The situation happened so fast that I think we were all left with a feeling of surprise.

I then glanced at Fiona who was wearing her night clothes, dressing gown and an odd pair of Wellington boots. It was so gloriously incongruous that I smiled and took her in my arms and kissed her warmly. She did not understand everything that had just happened and said, 'Oh Jack, you're absolutely soaked!'

'That's what you get if you wander around Salisbury Plain at night in torrential rain,' I said.

'Carolyn and I were worried to death about you both,' she replied.

While Paul was helping Loader get to his feet, I roughly grabbed the unconscious Mazuchelli and pulled him upright and checked him for any other weapons. Loader turned to me and said with great difficulty, 'You needn't have pushed me so damned hard, Jack.'

'Sorry about that. But at least I didn't hit you on the jaw, did I?' I said sarcastically.

'Thank God for that! You have a ruddy wicked punch,' he replied, glancing at Mazuchelli, who was now coming round and rubbing his face and moaning.

Suddenly another of the bells started clanging and I realised that the thug on the bell rope was trying to escape, but unsuccessfully. The big front door flew open again and three burly figures rushed in. I recognised them as the three who rescued us from our episode high up on the Clifton Suspension Bridge.

'You can leave it all to us now, Mr Loader,' said the first man, who was obviously the senior of the three.

'Thanks for coming so promptly,' Loader replied dryly. It was his feeble attempt at humour. He wasn't renowned for his wit in the Department.

There was an ugly sound of crashing timber as a figure slid down the bell rope and landed heavily on the flagstone floor in the bell tower, screaming out in pain as he landed. I had little sympathy with his predicament. The men who had come to our aid were, I assumed, Special Branch. They rounded them up and took them all away. I suspected that there was still at least one man missing, possibly more.

We all stood around catching our breath and senses. Paul was the first to speak and invited us back to the Vicarage after he had collected the oak box from the vestry and handed it to me.

Before the whole village became fully awake – and curious because of the noise we had created with the bells and the gunfire – we quickly walked back to the Vicarage, with me tightly holding the precious box. This time we made sure the Church was definitely locked.

We cleared the table in the front room, pulled the curtains together and looked at the incredible calligraphy and artwork of the pre-medieval period. It was written in Latin in Insular Uncial style, which none of us could translate because it was in religious Latin. So apart from the stunning workmanship, we didn't know exactly what we were looking at, except for the incredible pictorial pages.

Fiona was very interested because she had never, so she exclaimed, seen calligraphy and artwork like this at first hand before. Loader on the other hand, was wandering around, shaking his head in disbelief and smiling in triumph.

He finally said, 'You did it Jack! You actually did it!' And then he said, 'We must go to the Bodleian Library in Oxford and show the pages to Professor Watson-Young for final verification with carbon dating as soon as possible.'

He seemed to have only one thought in his mind, and took out his phone impulsively and rang the Bodleian Library. He had completely forgotten the hour. It was much too early and there was only a message saying that the Library would be open at 9 a.m. Loader rang later only to find out that the Professor was in Dublin at Trinity College, refreshing his knowledge of the *Book of Kells*.

We were all disappointed, Loader most of all, because he wanted to share this success and pass on the good news, although without verification I still wasn't too sure. 'The Professor will be back tomorrow. I have made a lunchtime appointment for us at the Bodleian Library.'

'May I suggest we get some rest? We have had a very disturbed night,' murmured Paul. We all agreed immediately.

Paul also mentioned he had to think of an inspiring sermon, as it was Sunday tomorrow, but because of the recent events it was going to be extremely difficult to find a subject to talk about which would be relevant to everyday and ordinary situations after all the excitement of the previous night.

'I have a small booklet from the Dean of St Asaph,' I said 'Or at least an account of the history about the Monastery of Kells, and how the book was stolen from there, found days later and eventually brought to Trinity College

Dublin for safe keeping from the Vikings. It was a copy of a book written by Bishop Tanner.'

Paul thought about it for a moment. 'That's a good idea. But do you think it's wise under the circumstances?'

'I don't think it will do any harm, so long as you don't mention Imber,' I replied with a sly wink.

'Imber? What's this about Imber?' interrupted Loader, who would have read a great deal of detail about the desolate village in government documents.

'I will tell you the modern up-to-date history tomorrow as we go to Oxford. I'm so tired. I have to rest,' I said swiftly, avoiding his question.

Fiona then spoke up. 'Could I ask a big favour of you both? I have followed your quest Jack, very closely from the time I met you in mid-Wales. My camera is in the car. It won't take me a moment to get it.'

I couldn't forget her courageous action when picking me up when I was in serious trouble on the English and Welsh border. It was obvious what she was asking, so I glanced at Loader for affirmation. He nodded and smiled at her, then he shrugged his shoulders.

'I didn't hear a thing, I'm going to bed,' he said with a strange smile.

We went out to her car to get her camera and all her equipment. She set it up as I watched in admiration. I drew out the pages slowly for her, one by one, and set them on her special stand.

There were about thirty pages in all, but as I drew out the last one from the leather pouch an old yellowed piece of paper fluttered to the floor. It was obviously written by Bishop Tanner – the writing was very shaky and dated August 8th 1735, a few months before his demise. In the note it said that he believed these magnificent pages could be the missing part of the *Book of Kells* and should be, and must be, sent to Trinity College Dublin. He had signed it with his distinctive initials.

I recognised the Bishop's writing from before, and there was no doubt in my mind now that these were what we had so fervently hoped to find. We packed everything away and took Fiona's camera equipment and the box up to my bedroom which I was sharing with Loader. I must confess I'd have rather shared with Fiona, but under the circumstances it wasn't possible.

As I lay in bed trying to rest, my mind went over the sequence of the day's events until I came to the last part, where Fiona was taking the close-up photographs of the pages. I realised that the pages looked different from the colour reproductions in modern books I had seen, because the margins around the work were much wider.

I was troubled by this. Were these really the pages I had been searching for? Everything seemed to point to this. Or were they merely work that been created much later in the ancient Celtic style?

This was possible, as even in modern times artists and calligraphers who admired the work still recreated work following the examples in the *Book of Kells* and other famous medieval manuscripts. I was not a world expert historian like the Professor at the Bodleian, so I turned over and slept lightly, because of the troublesome query in my brain; and in spite of Bishop Tanner's confident note.

One or two of the vellum pages were clearly minutely and skilfully altered with a cuttlefish, and this was also a possible clue to their origin, but only an expert would be able to tell me. Modern day vellum costs a small fortune and will last for centuries, but these pages were obviously extremely old.

SECRETS REVEALED

Sleep was difficult. The house was silent, then suddenly there was a tremendous noise at the back of the house, which sounded like something heavy falling down. A shattering of glass was followed by a piercing scream from Fiona. Loader was up immediately. He was still in his day clothes and we rushed down the corridor towards Fiona's bedroom and burst in. She was shaking like a leaf and clearly upset.

'What happened?' I said as I rushed towards her and put a comforting arm around her.

'A thick-set man with dark hair tried to get in the window, so I slammed the window down hard onto his hand and he fell backwards.'

'Well done,' I said. 'Are you sure you're all right?' She nodded and said, 'Yes.'

Loader meanwhile had rushed downstairs and round to the back of the house and shouted up, 'Nothing here. Just a broken ladder.'

I rushed down the stairs and out through the front door. I got to the metal front gate only to see a limping figure about to get into the big car opposite. He turned enough for me to see his face in the street light as he got into the car and drove away. I cursed silently, because I realised it was the one who had thumped me on the road from Rome to Venice. We had obviously not captured all of them, so we were still vulnerable, and more importantly, so was the box and the recovered missing pages.

When I returned to the Vicarage front door, Paul and his wife Carolyn by now were up and full of questions. I answered some of their queries about the attempted break in. They were quite worried but I told them that I had seen the offender drive off.

Fiona asked if she could sleep in my bedroom for her protection, and I gladly agreed. Loader meanwhile was making a temporary repair to the broken pane of glass with a sheet of cardboard. I made Fiona comfortable with a hug and a kiss and didn't let go until she stopped shaking. She had a small fleck of blood on her cheek which I hoped was his, not hers.

Finally, we all settled down to sleep after I checked all the doors, windows and Fiona's camera equipment and of course, the oak box with its valuable contents.

Early the following morning the good folk of the village were full of questions in the road outside the Vicarage. Fiona's scream of surprise would be heard quite clearly for a considerable distance. It was now early Sunday morning, which meant that Paul had to take the 10 o'clock morning service and the Evensong service at 6 o'clock, and couldn't come with us to Oxford. He was extremely disappointed, but I assured him his part in the quest would not go unrecognised.

There was a small and curious crowd gathering in the street in front of the Vicarage – which was the last thing I wanted. The one awful possibility was that the local press might turn up, so I turned to Paul and suggested he talk to them. He went out to the front gate and spoke quietly to the swiftly gathering crowd.

'Thank you for coming this morning, which we appreciate. As some of you know the Church was broken into and vandalised, and an unsuccessful attempt was made to break in to the Vicarage last night. I am happy to say we were not hurt. And nothing was stolen.'

A loud booming voice came from the back of the crowd. 'What about the blinking bells, Reverend?' said a concerned member of the bell ringers team. 'The platform is smashed, and the police have roped off the bell tower so we can't ring the bells.'

'Thank you, Bert, for pointing that out,' said Paul looking hopefully at Loader, who nodded his head slightly and said a quiet, 'Yes.'

'I can assure you the platform will be repaired properly before next Sunday,' said Paul.

'Thank you, Reverend' said Bert.

Before the crowd drifted slowly away, Paul took the opportunity to mention that the services would be at the normal times.

'Thank you, Paul,' I whispered as we went inside. 'I don't want the press here this morning – or ever if possible.'

'That's right,' he murmured. 'At least, not until you have gone to the Bodleian library in Oxford.'

As we sat down in the front room, there was a tap on the Vicarage door. It was the Matron and she and Paul had a quiet conversation in the hallway. Paul invited her in to the front room and introduced her to Loader. The Matron looked inquiringly at us and said, 'Did you have any luck in Imber?'

I smiled and said, 'Yes, we think we have found the missing pages. But we have to go to the Bodleian Library for verification. Thank you for your tremendous help. Can I rely on your silence for the time being? It really is very important.'

'I understand completely,' she said, with sincerity. Paul then said, 'Perhaps Matron would like to tell you how she was able to help us.'

Loader remained silent. Although he had warmly congratulated me earlier on my achievement, it seemed possible he was having nervous doubts again about the mention of Imber. Matron Grandville looked around the room at us and began to tell us some of what she had confided in Paul the other evening.

She explained, 'Briefly, one of our very elderly residents told me a story about her ancestors and also one of her brothers who had, like so many other young men in the early days of World War Two, been called up to fight for King and country.'

She said there had for many generations, been a box in the family. It had been kept secret and so before the young brother went off to the war in France, he had hidden the family's secret box in the lonely village on Salisbury Plain.

'As this lady now has no living relatives, she told me her story. When you came, Mr Harrison, looking for something in the nursing home, I thought I should tell the Reverend some of what the old lady had told me. I did not tell Paul the name of the family,' she said firmly, and then continued.

'I was happy to be able to help you, but please never reveal where you found your information – the old lady would be devastated. She would be most concerned that the family name would be known.'

Finally she said, 'Can I rely on your discretion?' We all agreed most profoundly.

The Matron accompanied Paul to church for morning service that day. I wished him well, and also noticed an increasing number of people wending their way to the Church. The bells calling the people to worship didn't ring that Sunday – this silence hadn't happened since the Second World War.

It was an eager group that sat in Loader's vehicle for the ride to Oxford, when a car pulled up alongside and out of the front passenger seat leapt Captain Stewart, although I didn't recognise him at first because he was wearing civilian clothes. He ran over to us and spoke to me while I sat in the driver's seat.

'Is the Vicar available? Because I want to give him some good news about the shell hole in Imber Church.'

'He is preparing for the morning service in the church,' I said.

'Ah, it's just that I wanted to tell him the good news about the shell hole – it will be repaired by the Army at their cost. And also the marble tomb, which appears to have been slightly damaged, too.'

At this point I felt it was time to put him in the picture about a few things, so I suggested we all returned quickly to the Vicarage. Loader was not happy about this idea, because he had the bit between his teeth and was eager to get to Oxford.

I told Captain Stewart the real truth about Imber. He expressed total surprise and then told us about his armed troops who had been instructed to patrol the whole area. There were two men asleep and two on duty watch.

The two men on duty were supposed to watch the radar screen, but were in fact playing cards when Paul and I entered the prohibited zone of Imber.

'I threatened to put them on a charge,' said Captain Stewart 'if they so much as mentioned the whole business. My daily report contained nothing out of the ordinary, which of course was usual,' he said with a grin. 'Now I am off duty for a two-week period. My wife is expecting me today in London.'

I looked at Loader, because he was silent and obviously planning something. He was a wily and cunning old devil, and he looked at me and said, 'What do you think? Perhaps we could do with the extra manpower?'

He turned to Captain Stewart and said, 'Do you have a gun?'

'No – I don't,' he said. 'Not when I'm off duty, thank you.'

Loader turned to the others and said, 'Excuse us for a moment please.' Turning to me he said, 'Would you come with me into the kitchen Jack.' I followed him into the kitchen.

'What do you think of Captain Stewart?' he said in a whisper.

'I like him,' I said equally quietly.

'That wasn't what I was asking you,' he replied angrily.

'No, of course not. What you were really asking is, can he be trusted?' I replied just as strongly.

'Yes exactly. There are far too many people involved already, for my liking.'

At that moment Captain Stewart entered the kitchen unannounced. 'Please excuse me. I realise that you don't know me as well as you might, but I would like to allay your fears, by telling you about myself.'

'Yes, please do. But very briefly. We are now very short of time,' Loader replied.

'I was born and raised in Altrincham, went to Manchester Grammar School and Manchester University. I got a science degree and after a time joined the Army. I have been in Military Service for 10 years and worked in security at all levels. I can, if required, give you names and clearance information.'

For some reason Loader seemed very happy with this answer, and then I remembered he also had been to Manchester University. If this satisfied him, it was alright with me.

'Well, that's fine,' I said quickly. 'Let's get on our way.'

We all went out to Loader's car. It was agreed that I should drive, because I knew the way, and because Loader's right arm was still painful from my necessary vicious action in the Church. However, he sat in the front passenger seat with the box under his long legs to cover it. Fiona and Captain Stewart sat in the rear seat.

Fiona was now more relaxed and had her feelings under control, but contributed little to the conversation. Captain Stewart was full of questions which Loader answered tersely. I sensed his reluctance to give away too much information.

I drove as fast as the speed limit would allow – we were behind schedule. Conversation was limited as we sped along.

We reached the M4 motorway and then turned north to Oxford. I had kept an eye open for any vehicles following. I was held up by slow moving traffic and behind me was a furniture van which effectively blocked my rear vision.

Suddenly the traffic cleared, the furniture van turned off to the left and exposed the large limousine right behind us. Loader noticed this too, and warned me with a shout and wound his window down. The limousine quickly drew alongside and tried unsuccessfully to drive us off the road. The driver drew alongside again and then brought me to a screeching halt by the side of the road. Two men leapt out. Loader had brought out a pistol from somewhere and fired a shot with his left hand. The driver of the other vehicle almost simultaneously fired back and made a dent in the roof above my head.

That decided my next action. I rammed the lever into low gear, trod hard on the accelerator and swung the wheel over. Travelling at speed, I charged hard at the open door of the limousine while Loader was shouting angrily.

'No, Jack!' he screamed,' not with my ruddy car you don't! You crazy bastard!'

'No choice,' I shouted back. There was an unpleasant noise of grinding metal as I completely tore off the driver's front door. The door flew up in the air and landed in front of an oncoming builder's truck which flattened it, although the driver tried unsuccessfully to avoid it.

All three of us jumped out as I came to a halt and dived towards the limousine to disarm them – they had thrown themselves into the front seats to avoid being mowed down by our car.

Meanwhile, the builder's truck had come to a shuddering halt, with brakes screaming. It happened so quickly, but it didn't stop Loader venting his anger at me for ruining his car. While Loader pointed his pistol at them, I disarmed them. They were shaken by the events of my violent and speedy action. Loader then put a bullet in one of the front tyres for good measure.

'That will slow them down a bit,' he muttered viciously.

'They couldn't go very fast anyway, with a missing door,' I returned.

'No. But it'll take a while to change the wheel,' he retorted.

'That's true. But what about the truck driver?'

'No doubt he will report the incident to the police – in fact, that's what he's doing right now by the look of it.'

I looked down the road and sure enough, the truck had stopped about 50 metres away. 'Right, that settles it, we must hurry. Let's get going,' I said.

The truck driver had stopped, got out and was using his phone, then he started to move quickly towards us, shouting obscenities. 'I've got your bloody number!' he shouted.

We hadn't time for a chat, so we drove off hurriedly. Loader was still cursing about the damage to his car. Fiona remained silent as we continued on to Oxford. She obviously didn't enjoy the violent action of mine, I sadly realised.

CHAPTER 15

MODERN TECHNOLOGY

As we arrived at the entrance of the Bodleian Library, Professor Watson-Young appeared at the main door almost immediately and directed us to his parking spot.

'Use my spot. I came by taxi today. Thank you, Mr Loader for calling me about your expected time of arrival.'

We followed him inside and hurried through the foyer and along to his office. He was very thrilled to see us but was more excited at the prospect of seeing what we had brought.

'Now, what have you found for me?' he said, rubbing his hands together with anticipation.

Loader, who had carried the wooden box, laid it down on the large table at the nearest end. He carefully unwrapped it, showing the date of 1668. The box now looked much more interesting, having been thoroughly cleaned by Carolyn.

The Professor didn't say a word, but his hands were shaking with excitement. He handed me some white cotton gloves to use. As I drew each page out with great care, he expressed enormous delight and wonderment. He gently placed each one on the table, until all of them were side by side around the large table. I then showed him the note that Fiona and I had discovered from Bishop Thomas Tanner dated 8th August 1735.

He read the note carefully twice and then finally said, 'Ah well, the dear Bishop was confident these are the missing pages. However, he doesn't explain why. Or for that matter, how they came into his possession. Perhaps we will never know.'

'No, that's true,' I said. 'But with modern technology we might learn more about these pages.'

'That's why I flew to Dublin so hurriedly,' he replied. 'To have another glimpse at the *Book of Kells* and refresh my memory. They kindly allowed me to take several photographs with my digital camera so that I could compare them with what you have found.'

As he spoke, he looked at all the pages around the table, carefully studying each one in turn, and then going back round again and again. We remained silent as he did this, wondering what he was thinking. Finally he took out a measuring tape, a plastic ruler and a small pair of stainless steel scissors. He compared each page, measured each one across the width and finally put a green marker near three that he had chosen.

'Now we are getting to the difficult part,' he murmured. 'You see, I have to choose some of these to cut, for a very small sample of the vellum for testing by radio carbon dating. Do you understand?'

I was a little tense at this point. We nodded as if we agreed with him and understood, but of course not quite – he was the top expert after all.

The stillness continued as the Professor moved silently around the table with his white cotton gloves, muttering quietly to himself and occasionally wiping his forehead.

He was totally unaware of our presence as his mind was concentrating on the important decision. His bushy eyebrows were moving up and down with surprise and delight as he moved around the table. Then, as if he had finally come to a decision, he went to a cupboard and brought out a rather impressive stereo microscope and looked at one of the three he had chosen. He turned to me and said with a look of triumph.

'Perhaps, as you are the calligrapher Jack – you might like to look at the beautiful script.'

I was flattered at being called 'the calligrapher' and I certainly wasn't going to pass up this golden opportunity.

The detail was amazing, even at low magnification. The minutiae and crispness of the workmanship was heart stopping. I could almost feel the texture of the vellum, considering the possible age of the manuscript, because it was so much more exciting to see the real thing. Although the colour photographs in calligraphy sample books were very good – even excellent – they just could not compare with studying the original work.

I had stepped sideways to allow Fiona to have the next close look, when there was a knocking on the door. The Professor tut-tutted with exasperation and disbelief.

'No one is allowed in here at any time now. Especially today!' he said angrily.

Loader took the initiative at once, striding across to the door and opening it enough to speak through the gap. There was a muffled conversation, then Loader turned round and said, 'It's for me. Don't concern yourselves,' and left silently.

I guessed it was something to do with his vehicle and the accident, although it wasn't an accident, but was a deliberate action on my part. While Loader was out of the room, the Professor gave us a short discourse on the history of the *Book of Kells*, most of which I knew, but it was a pleasure to hear it from an expert who must surely have given well attended and popular lectures in Oxford.

'The book is now in Trinity College, Dublin, rebound into four volumes. Sadly, on one of the re-bindings in pre-Victorian times, it was trimmed in a foolish attempt to straighten the edges. Some experts believe it was planned or created first on the Isle of Iona off the West Scottish coast. The Vikings raided Iona in 807AD and so the Book was perhaps moved by the Monks to the Kells monastery, in County Meath in Ireland.'

He paused then continued, 'But it's still not historically certain where it was begun.

'The Book appeared in their records before the time of the Norman Conquest in the Chapter House at Kells – that the great Gospel *Book of Kells* was stolen for its gold and jewel encrusted cover in 1006 A.D.' The Professor stopped briefly and studied us. He saw that he had our full attention and continued.

'The pages were brutally ripped out and found days later in an Irish peat bog. The Abbey was then plundered by Vikings in the 10th century but somehow survived. Gerald of Wales almost certainly saw the book later in the 12th century and it stayed in Kells until 1654, when Oliver Cromwell's cavalry was stabled in the Monastery. After the restoration of the Monastery by Queen Elizabeth I, it was sent to Trinity College, Dublin for safety.' He stopped again and watched Fiona as she made copious notes.

'However,' he continued, 'In the year 2000, one volume of the Gospel of St Mark was sent to Canberra in Australia for an exhibition of illuminated manuscripts. Sadly, it suffered minor pigment damage. It was reported in some newspapers and is believed to have been caused by engine vibrations on the long flight.' He paused again. 'And so if these pages are what we all hope they are, they cannot go by air to Dublin.'

'Does that mean we have to get them there by boat? Across the Irish Sea?' I said.

'Yes,' he said emphatically. 'I must insist on it in case of similar damage.'

At that moment Loader returned. 'Sorry, Professor. May I have a private word with Mr Harrison outside?' he said, with an angry motion of his head.

We went out and he explained furiously that the week-end porter or security guard had called the police, because he noticed a stranger's car in the Professor's parking spot; and the car was seriously damaged.

'What did the police say?' I asked, slightly troubled.

'I managed to clear it with them and showed them my identification and my senior position in the Government. They had noticed the damage to the front of the car. I explained about the crash, and how we had no choice because we were in serious danger. I also handed them one of the guns we had taken, but kept one of them for us, just in case we needed a loaded gun. I also pointed out to them it was an Italian Beretta, which I suspected was not registered in Britain and brought in illegally.'

'So the police are on our side, and fully briefed about us?'

'Yes. I told them to contact the Wiltshire police for details of the incident at the Church at Market Lavington, but not the deserted village of Imber.'

'Thanks for that,' I replied, somewhat relieved. 'And what about the three crooks at the Church?'

'They will be kept in custody by Special Branch on charges of illegal entry, damage to church property, and discharging a firearm in the Church. And possibly attempted murder.'

'You did a good job, Loader,' I said without any sarcasm. He pulled a wry face and said, 'I haven't forgiven you for the damage you did to my car, you reckless clot.'

'Well, let's have another look at it,' I replied. 'It's probably not as bad as you imagine.'

'Huh! You ruddy well hope so!' he fired back.

We went back outside to the car park as the police were about to leave, but annoyingly pointed out the damage to the top of the windscreen and the roof. I was hoping Loader wouldn't say anything, but of course he did.

'You realise this is my car, not the Department's?' he roared. 'So the repairs will come out of your expense account.'

'That's hardly fair,' I said.' You were there too when it happened.'

'The Department knows nothing about this whole business. At least officially,' he retorted quickly.

'So if it all goes wrong, and I didn't find the missing pages, then you and the Department are in the clear?' I said angrily.

'Exactly! You've hit the nail on the head. Because I was on leave in Australia and had an accident, which put me into hospital in Hobart and officially I am still there. That's the Department's story.'

'Talking of money – where is my money coming from? You told me this would be easy but nothing could be further from the truth. You flattered me about my knowledge and used my connection with calligraphy as a lever to get my interest and co-operation.'

'I did not tell you it would be easy, but your father told me you were "nuts about calligraphy". That was his expression, if I remember correctly.'

'So it's my father's fault, is it? You certainly know how to shift the blame,' I said.

'Yes. Did you know he has an interesting collection of 14th and 15th century documents, books and illuminated pages?'

'Yes, of course I did. But you still haven't answered my question about my money.'

'The Prime Minister is now fully briefed on your part. If we are successful, we go to No 10 Downing Street soon to show him the pages. After we leave here, so don't worry about the damn money.'

'When do we leave?' I said hopefully.

'That's up to Professor Watson-Young. If he's convinced they're genuine, it's all systems go,' he replied.

'I'm going back in to see the Professor,' I said with determination.

'No you're not!' he said angrily and pointed to the rear view mirror – it was completely missing from the crumpled front area. I had noticed it earlier, but had said nothing in the hope that he wouldn't blow his top.

'You'll have to pay for that!' he roared through his clenched teeth. He still had his jaw wired together.

It was not surprising he was bad tempered; he couldn't eat properly and I realised it was wearing him down. Although I was pretty confident we had achieved our goal, it had taken its toll on him. Trying to cheer him up I promised to pay for repairs to his car.

'Come on let's go inside and see what the latest is. It could be good news,' I said hopefully. Although he didn't seem convinced he reluctantly came in with me.

When we entered the room there was an air of excitement, especially from Fiona who grabbed my arm and whispered in my ear and kissed me on the cheek. I took this sign as a positive one and whispered to her, 'Would you do something for me?'

'Yes, of course Jack. What is it?' she said.

'Go and cheer up Loader. He's a very upset with me about the car,' I said.

'That's not what I was expecting you to ask,' she replied with a cheeky smile.

Loader was sitting alone on one of the elegant mahogany chairs situated around the oak panelled room. Fiona was the only person who could work miracles with him and he was too much of a gentleman to be impolite to her, so it might work. Fiona walked across and started chatting to him and I turned my attention back to the Professor Watson-Young who was busy studying the pages.

Suddenly the Professor stopped, straightened up and spoke.

'May I have your attention please?' He then paused and smiled at us, paused again for effect, to make sure we were listening, which of course we were. He then continued, 'I am confident that what we have here is the real thing, so I am ringing Professor Damian Fitzmaurice of Trinity College, Dublin – right away.'

In an exaggerated movement, he picked up the phone, pressed a number, and put it on speaker phone. We watched silently while he drummed his fingers on the table.

'Ah! Fitz, my friend. How would you like afternoon tea at my house tomorrow?'

There was a long pause at the other end of the line and a distinguished voice in a soft Irish accent said, 'Really! That's very nice of you – are you sure?'

'Yes, I am sure. I think you will enjoy yourself. What shall it be: tennis or croquet?'

'Well, if you're sure. I'd love to come. I think it had better be croquet at my age,' was the excited reply.

No more was said, and the Professor put down the phone and grinned at us. This was obviously a prearranged speech. 'Now, we have to remain calm and not speak to anyone about this,' he said in an emphatic stage whisper.

'What about the samples you have taken – the slivers of vellum?' I said.

'Goodness! In my excitement I almost forgot.' He picked up the phone again and called. 'Is that you Frank? I have a little project for you. Can you come to see me promptly at 9 o'clock tomorrow? I think you will find what I have for you extremely interesting.'

So saying, he very carefully put the tiny samples into special archival envelopes. We watched him closely. Captain Stewart cleared his throat and requested to look through the microscope. Loader was the next to look, which obviously impressed him. As he straightened up, his demeanour changed and he glanced at me and inclined his head with a smile of triumph.

We still couldn't be sure, however, that we had found the pages, and so I asked the Professor, 'How long will it take the scientists to get a result with the radio carbon dating?' I said.

'Ah! Since the development of this very special science we have improved greatly, not only the accuracy, but the length of time taken. But I don't want to put pressure on them to get a quick result. You see, we want as accurate a date as possible, because I am unable at this point to tell them what this is all about.'

He looked around at us in turn for some comment. We were silent as we thought our private thoughts, except Fiona who was looking at me with a look of admiration and then walked towards me and squeezed my hand.

The room was silent, so I said, 'What happens next, Professor?'

'We all deserve a glass of the finest champagne, don't you think?' he replied.

Captain Stewart murmured something in agreement about having a dry throat. We all agreed.

The Professor gently put all the pages back in the box and into the secure locked room. A taxi was called for him and we all followed him out to his charming Georgian mansion in the countryside. As we drove through the streets of Oxford with the warm summer sun on the ancient buildings, I thought how fantastic they looked. It was easy to understand why Oxford was called the 'City of Dreaming Spires'.

Loader asked me how many thugs were still out there to be of concern to us. To which I could not give an accurate answer. 'Probably three or more. But as we have no idea just who we are dealing with, who knows?' I said. Loader groaned quietly.

The Professor and his charming wife Patricia happily entertained us. We felt satisfied with our day's work; even Loader smiled at Fiona. Captain Stewart, although not fully understanding what he had become involved in, caught the atmosphere, was laughing and then asked to be excused to ring his wife in London. I reminded him quietly not to let anything slip. I deliberately stepped in before Loader could say something to him.

'Can you make up some plausible story before you speak to her, something about car trouble perhaps?' I suggested.

He thought about it and before he replied, Loader butted in and reminded him also not to mention where we were. I listened in to Captain

Stewart's conversation at a polite distance, but although he said all the right things he didn't seem to convince her entirely.

We were on the terrace at the rear of the Professor's mansion, surrounded by exotic trees of all description and beautifully landscaped. The land sloped away gently from the house and in the distance there were cattle grazing quietly in the field. It was such an idyllic country scene and it reminded me very much of my hobby farm in Tasmania. I thought that I should call Peter Morris soon, at least to keep him up to date.

After toasting our success with champagne, the Professor and his wife entertained us with traditional Devonshire tea of scones, cream and home made raspberry jam, plus tea and coffee. We were a merry party, but in spite of our jollity, I still had lingering doubts and so did Loader until the carbon dating results were known. We had to wait at least two days, maybe longer, so I thought, what could we do to amuse ourselves and keep out of harm's way?

We broke up into separate parties to admire the garden, which relaxed us all. Fiona and I deliberately walked to the very bottom of the garden and hid in a dense group of trees. We were obviously thinking alike – we wanted to be alone.

We stopped between two magnificent Lombardy poplar trees, making sure we could not be seen. I took her in my arms, held her around the waist and kissed her passionately. She responded warmly, but then stopped suddenly, with a sharp intake of breath as if I had hurt her. I looked into her face and she was staring into the sunken ditch behind the stone wall.

'What's that?' she said nervously. I looked down to see what was troubling her.

'It's called a haha,' I replied, as quietly as I could try to calm her. 'The stone wall is designed to keep cattle out and not spoil the view from the house or garden.'

'That's not what I'm referring to, silly,' she said softly. 'What's he doing there?' emphasising the word 'he.'

I looked down again and along the wide ditch and saw a man with a gun who made a signal with one finger over his lips. I sat down on the top of the wall and invited Fiona to do the same. 'What the hell are you doing here?' I said to him. 'You scared the life out of my girlfriend.'

'Sorry, Mr Harrison, you'd better talk to Mr Loader. Besides there's two of us,' he replied swiftly.

I looked along the sunken ditch in the other direction to confirm, and sure enough, he was right. It was sensible of Loader to bring back-up, but he should have informed me. We walked casually back to the house as the dinner gong sounded.

Once again the Professor and his wife entertained us very well, as he took the head of the table with Loader on his right and myself on his left, Fiona next to me opposite the Professor's wife. The two ladies talked freely. Mrs Watson-Young was fascinated by Fiona's work and the story of her recent visit to Portmeirion. Fiona was a convivial conversationalist and kept the party amused.

The Professor was in good humour too, but Loader was either tired or worried about something. It was then I realised he was still concerned about the safety of the whole project. I whispered in Fiona's ear, asking for a pen and a scrap of paper. I wrote a note about the guards and slid it across the table to him while the party was listening to the Professor, who was holding forth once again about the book. Loader brightened up considerably after that. Finally the party split up for some well earned rest.

Without making a big issue about it the Professor put Fiona and me together in one bedroom, Loader in another and Captain Stewart in another. We all slept very soundly in the most comfortable beds.

CHAPTER 16

A NARROW ESCAPE

There had been a sharp shower of rain in the early morning, which made everything in the garden a sparkling green. I looked out of the perfectly proportioned Georgian window on to the beautiful gardens and realised in that moment that I was extremely content. I looked back towards the bed where Fiona was sleeping soundly. She was so beautiful I wanted to wake her and hold her in my arms, but thought better of it and let her sleep on in peace. I looked down the garden and caught a glimpse of the two armed figures, which also made me feel much safer.

After breakfast we went our separate ways. The Professor went with a guard to the Bodleian Library and then to the airport to pick up Professor Damian Fitzmaurice from Dublin. Loader went with the other guard to the hospital to have his jaw unwired – which I found out later. This left Fiona and me with Captain Stewart with time on our hands.

Fiona thought we should go shopping, so we called a taxi and asked him to take us to near the Westgate Shopping Complex in Oxford. He dropped us off in the High Street and we strolled towards the shopping area.

Oxford was so rich in history, it was a delight to just walk through the streets like tourists, enjoying its historic buildings. I appreciated Captain Stewart's presence; he was looking for a piece of jewellery for his wife and asked Fiona's advice. I also bought a beautiful Celtic brooch for Fiona, because I thought she deserved something special. We were all enjoying ourselves, although I was still keeping a wary eye out for trouble – I still couldn't let my guard down. We chose a pleasant coffee shop in a quiet corner and I positioned myself so that I could see the entrance door.

We chatted away amicably, covering many subjects, but not about the book. Captain Stewart told us about his gunnery knowledge and other explosives, chemical warfare, trajectory of rockets; plus a lot more of which I only had a basic grasp, and Fiona had even less.

For my part, I lightened the conversation by telling them about Tasmania, its history, beautiful beaches, rugged landscape, mountains and lakes. Fiona described her passion for architecture and photography.

We were all totally relaxed when the entrance door to the coffee shop opened and three swarthy looking men walked in. I realised immediately who they were. The other customers went very quiet for a moment, as they cast a suspicious eye over them and having assessed them, resumed their conversations. I didn't move and neither did Captain Stewart. Fiona, however, was caught in mid-sentence.

They stopped and looked around the room, obviously spotted us, then turned and went out. I breathed a sigh of relief, but they looked back in through the glass door as if to make sure it was us and then disappeared. Captain Stewart turned to me and muttered quietly without any obvious apprehension, 'What do you suggest we do now?'

I thought for a moment and said, 'We do nothing. We stay here, enjoy our teacakes and finish our coffee, catch a taxi and ask him to drive around Oxford like normal tourists. Hopefully we'll lose them in the process, then circle back to the Professor's house.'

We paid our bill and sauntered out of the shopping centre, but as we got closer to the taxi rank, we increased our stride until we were almost running, grabbed the first taxi and asked him how well he knew Oxford.

'Very well. Lived here all my life,' he replied cheerfully in the local accent.

'Good. Could you take us around to some of the famous buildings. Except the Bodleian Library. We've seen that,' I answered.

My plan was to lose them in the process if we were being followed, and that's exactly what happened, each one of us keeping careful watch in turn. Finally, we returned to the Professor's mansion via Iffley Road on our way to the south-east corner of the County.

As we drove into the wide sweeping driveway, Professor Watson-Young greeted us graciously at the porticoed front door. He was cheerful, because Professor Fitzmaurice had arrived from Dublin, and they were plainly excited at the prospect of our collective success. We were formally introduced to the Irish Professor and went happily into the extensive library, where we sat down comfortably talking about many subjects, especially learning of Dublin from Professor Fitzmaurice. We were all interested to learn about Dublin.

The two Professors chatted away confidently, firm in their belief that we had the missing pages; we listened almost silently in awe as they expounded their broad knowledge of the subject.

Suddenly Loader appeared, his face looked different and he spoke clearly without any difficulty. He now had the wire bracing removed from his jaw and was in a much better frame of mind. I was happy for him, and relieved.

We listened to the experts discussing the *Book of Kells* and the strong possibility that the pages I had found in my quest were indeed the treasure that we all hoped for; but only the radio carbon dating could tell us the date.

I hoped that maybe tomorrow we would get the scientists' analysis, as only this would finally put our minds at rest.

We retired early to await developments, although I didn't sleep soundly. I woke at one point to look out of the window to see if we were still being looked after by the security guards – we were, so I went back to bed and at last slept peacefully.

The next morning after breakfast I drove Loader, Captain Stewart and Fiona in our car towards Oxford, while the two Professors with a driver and guard went in the other car. We originally planned to go to the Bodleian Library in two completely different directions, for safety. However, as I drove out of the gravel drive, a large dark limousine started to turn into the drive entrance and swerved around in front of us, showering us with gravel.

I did the same, but with a swift left hand turn turned away, putting my foot down hard and increased my speed towards Oxford. The Professor's car followed behind us for safety.

'Did you get the damned number?' I shouted.

'Yes, most of it,' replied Captain Stewart. 'It's a very new BMW, dark blue with a British number plate and a very recent registration. Should be easy to track down.'

'Thank you, Captain Stewart,' I said back. 'I'm really glad you joined us.'

'Call me David. We are now in this together. First names will do,' he replied.

It was a tense moment which could have ended very badly for us. Loader remained very tight lipped and said nothing. He obviously realised I had no choice under the circumstances.

There was a slight possibility we would have a result today from the radio carbon dating process, one way or the other, so I prayed for a positive result. In its long momentous history, the book deserved a happy conclusion.

We arrived at the Bodleian Library somewhat annoyed and shaken up, but in one piece and sat down in the Professor's office. We waited expectantly with him, the tension mounting. Time passed slowly and conversation was limited. Fiona whispered nervously to me. 'How long do you think we will have to wait?'

'I'm not sure' I replied. 'I'm not an expert on radio carbon dating, but we were advised to arrive before ten o'clock, which we did. Now it's a quarter past.'

The telephone suddenly burst into life. The Professor stood up and quietly answered, 'Watson-Young here,' and then pressed the button on the speaker phone for our benefit.

'Well, you're not going to believe this,' the excited voice said, 'but our first test strip gave us a date of approximately 750AD which was a surprise to us,' said the scientist. 'That's plus or minus 50 years, of course. The second strip gave us a slightly later reading, but still in the same era, plus or minus 50 years. We are testing the third strip this afternoon and will let you know this afternoon or later this evening.'

The Professor turned towards us with a broad smile and spoke into the phone. 'Thank you Frank, thank you very much, my friend.'

'Can I ask you what this is all about Thomas? You are being very secretive,' said the scientist. There was a long pause while the Professor pondered the question. He shook his head slowly. 'I think you will know the full answer next week.' He put the phone down before the voice could ask any more questions.

An air of expectation filled the room as we looked at one another, thinking our own thoughts. Loader was the first to break the silence.

'Thank you, Professor for not giving away too much information. I appreciate your discretion.' He went over to Thomas Watson Young, shook his hand and whispered something to him. They both turned towards the rest of us and thanked us for our magnificent effort. Loader seemed particularly pleased. Was this the end of the long search for me? The question that occurred to me however was the significance of the dates.

'So what can we conclude from these dates, Professor? I am slightly puzzled,' I said.

'Well,' he scratched his head thoughtfully and began to explain. 'Let's think – the dates are most interesting. You remember back in the history of the book it was stolen from the monastery at Kells? The exact date is uncertain, but thought to be 1006 or 1007 A.D. – before the time of the Norman Conquest in 1066.'

He paused again. 'So if these dates are confirmed they must be, I believe, written by skilled scribes for the original book. The slight variation in the dates could be as a result of when the vellum was actually prepared as a writing surface. It would be nice, wouldn't it, if we ever found the gold and jewel encrusted covers?'

At this point Professor Fitzmaurice spoke up in his quiet Irish voice. 'Wouldn't that be grand, but a lost cause I fear.' We all agreed. 'Possibly the Vikings again!' said the Professors almost in unison.

Loader then spoke up with a request. 'Could I tell the Prime Minister that we have found the missing pages, or not? You see it's essential that I report back as soon as possible.' The two Professors went into a huddled private conference at the far end of the room while we waited. Finally they came back after several minutes to sit down with us.

'We both now agree that these are the missing pages that were written probably at the Monastery of Kells. Or as some experts believe, started on the Scottish coast on the Isle of Iona circa 700- 800 A.D. or soon after. The clues that you, Jack have discovered' – with a gracious nod and a smile to me – 'all point to this conclusion.' Fiona glanced at me again. Then he continued, 'But how they got from the Monastery to the deserted 13th century church on the edge of Salisbury Plain is a complete mystery to us. Perhaps to remain a secret for ever,' he concluded.

I thought I should interrupt at this point. 'I may be able to partly explain how this might have happened. Bishop Tanner was a notable antiquarian, and had an extensive collection which you obviously know about. Perhaps he found the pages in his many travels in Ireland and Wales, but only suspected that they were the original pages. When his collection was transferred to the Bodleian, it is possible that somehow items could have been lost.

'With regard to the village of Imber, the fact is that the village is no longer on modern maps. And now only on old maps from the 1930s, even though very few of these still exist, which is rather sad. The villagers were asked to leave their homes without compensation of any sort, except a vague promise they could return after World War II. Sadly, this has not been the case. This is why it is now a ghost village and therefore it proved to be a perfect hiding place for the pages.'

At my explanation they all descended into a silence as we remembered the villagers who gave up their heritage for a higher cause, i.e. the D-Day landings and the freedom of the enslaved nations of Europe. I didn't tell them of the rumoured story about the American troops being allowed to train there in the village.

The telephone rang again and the Professor picked up the hand piece. 'Hello,' he said softly, 'oh it's you. I didn't expect a call quite so soon.' He waited while the person at the other end spoke. 'That's good – no it's magnificent news. Thank you very much,' he said and turned towards us with a smile that told us all that we had hoped. 'It's definite. The scientists are positive of the date.'

'Well, you can believe it now,' he continued.' That was the final result on the third sample and it's excellent news. This third result confirms our hopes. This calls for congratulations to all concerned, especially you, Jack. A most momentous development which will have far reaching effects on the history of the great book!'

We all thanked him, shook hands, piled into the cars and returned to the Professor's house. I was driving while Loader in the front passenger seat was phoning someone with the good news. I assumed he was speaking to someone in the government. He ended the phone conversation, turned towards me and said, 'The PM wants to see us tomorrow at 12.30 p.m. promptly.'

'How did he take the good news. Did you speak to the Prime Minister personally?' I said.

'He's thrilled to bits. Couldn't be happier and yes – I did speak to the PM,' was the triumphant reply.

At that moment a large car coming towards us swerved slightly into our path and then swerved away. It was one of the cars that had tried to stop me in Mid-Wales with its front end still damaged. So they were still mobile, I realised. There were three figures in the car, so the police hadn't caught all our opponents. I didn't say anything, but Loader had obviously noticed too. He cast a quick glance in my direction and remained grim faced.

Our satisfaction was boundless, but Loader and I knew the assignment wasn't quite finished. We had to take the pages to 10 Downing Street to the Prime Minister at the time he specified the next day, because of his duties in the House of Commons.

'How long will it take to get to Downing Street from here?' I said to Loader.

'Once you get onto the M40 Motorway it's almost straight in – just over an hour,' he said.

CONFIRMATION

We returned to the Professor's house and tried to relax, although we were very excited. I felt glad that my quest was almost complete. Fiona had a wonderful smile on her face and was once again the life and soul of the party. We couldn't be more contented with the scientific results. Loader was more relaxed than usual – his face was wreathed in smiles, although he whispered to me that he was a little bit nervous about the meeting tomorrow with the Prime Minister. I told him to stop worrying.

Fiona and I walked down the beautiful gardens, reached the end and sat down to talk about us. I wanted to be with her very much and wished to sound out her thoughts and feelings. My farm back in Tasmania might not be to her liking – perhaps she preferred to stay in Southern England, and carry on her career as a photographic journalist. I was, to say the least, tongue-tied and was unsure how to approach the subject.

She sensed my hesitation and changed the conversation to the pages we had found. I described to her my long journey and search through Italy. She laughed at certain parts of my story, which was encouraging.

Then I asked her, 'Would you like to come to visit me in Tasmania? It's a great place. You deserve a holiday and by the time we get there it will be early spring.'

She didn't answer immediately, but then gave me a long considered answer. 'Yes,' she said, 'but only for three weeks at the moment.'

This was a promising start, but I asked her rather sadly, why only three weeks? I was puzzled and then she clarified her thoughts by saying she had more work to finish because of everything that had happened. I then realised what I had thought subconsciously, that she really loved her work and was very dedicated and responsible. Well, having a professional attitude was fine with me – her enthusiasm for life and wide knowledge was what attracted me to her from the start of our acquaintance.

I remembered her incredible courage in picking me up in Mid-Wales when my spirits were at low ebb, with no car. She also unintentionally rescued the situation at the church in the middle of the night, coming into the church, with the Vicar's wife, at the right time and switching on the lights.

'I understand,' I said blankly, but was still uncertain of her thoughts. Suddenly, the situation changed and so did the conversation: Coming towards us, waving a letter was Professor Watson-Young, who said, 'It has a Devizes post-mark, so you should know who it's from.'

The only person it could be was the Reverend Paul Charlton from St Mary's Church. I opened the letter carefully; the handwriting on the address was in excellent italic and I started to read out loud.

> *The Vicarage*
> *Market Lavington*
> *'Dear Jack and Fiona,*
>
> *I have just received more information which I am sure will interest you. Gentle inquiries by the Matron brought out the following response from the dear lady who is now in her nineties.*
>
> *You will remember Bishop Tanner bequeathed all his papers to the Bodleian Library and some of the material was brought by barge along the River Thames and the Cherwell River.*
>
> *Sadly the barge had a navigational problem and partially sank near an island approaching Oxford. It was thought that all the contents were miraculously saved, but the box, being wood, floated away safely and was found the next day by the men who had been charged to look after the barge and its contents.*
>
> *The remarkable thing is it came to no harm, because the box was wrapped in 'Cerecloth' which is a waxed waterproof cloth of a kind sometimes used as a shroud in medieval times.*
>
> *Not knowing what to do and believing they were in serious trouble, the men returned with the box to Market Lavington to their families and kept it safe through successive generations. However, the family were worried at the beginning of World War Two when Britain was in imminent danger of invasion that the box would fall into the wrong hands. The family however, wisely took a set of photographs of the pages which they kept secretly in the village and one of the brothers then hid the original oak box with the pages in the marble tomb of the Rous family in Imber Church, obviously before December 1943 when the village was evacuated by the Army for training purposes.*

Sadly the brother did not return from the war and so the rest of the family were left with only a vague memory of the event. I am still unable to tell you the family name – my apologies.

My wife joins me in wishing you a safe and successful journey.'

Your good friend. Paul Charlton (Rev.)

I folded the letter, placed it back in the envelope and put it inside my jacket pocket. The Professor said, 'Well, that clarifies a little more of the mystery.' The three of us then walked slowly back to the house in silence.

Loader asked me to assist him and plan the next day's journey to London so there were no hold-ups or dangerous situations. We studied a large-scale roadmap carefully – although he knew the area well, he did not want any mistakes.

Just for safety's sake, he planned alternate routes in case we were ambushed. Detailed planning was his forte. He told me we would be accompanied by two police vehicles in ordinary standard colours, but heavily armed. All his previous experience pointed, he said, to this being a wise decision.

Captain Stewart agreed, but suggested that perhaps we should collect the box tonight and keep it under guard here at the house. Loader politely didn't agree with this plan; in his opinion it was perfectly safe where it was. This meant we had to start out half an hour earlier to collect the box.

Having meticulously planned our route and going through the route again and again, Loader felt satisfied with his plan. We retired early to get the maximum rest, because it was obviously going to be a long and arduous day.

LONDON V.I.P.

W
e rose early and set off eagerly in our cars for the Bodleian Library again, this time accompanied by the two police cars. I was satisfied we were now as safe as possible. We entered the Professor's secure room where Loader collected the precious box, and with the Professor and me on either side of him, we went out into the courtyard to the parked cars and placed the box carefully in our car, in front of the passenger seat. Loader insisted that he drove, which meant the box was hidden under my legs. The two police cars, meanwhile, were parked close by on duty.

There are many ways into London, although only one way into No.10 Downing Street. We became parted from one of the accompanying police cars on only one occasion at a set of traffic lights, but they easily caught up with us. It was a moment of slight concern, because it was the second police car at the rear, which left us vulnerable to attack from behind. Fortunately it didn't happen. Perhaps we were going to get a clear run into London.

We reached the central area of London and made our way to Downing Street, Loader driving carefully through the Whitehall area, which he knew extremely well, and finally arrived safely outside No 10 – the Prime Minister's house.

Climbing out of the car and with Loader's help, I carried the box nervously towards the famous black front door which opened as if by magic because of a TV camera and a custodian who is part of the 24-hour surveillance. We were ushered into the entrance hall with its black and white chequerboard floor, and then shown into the Cabinet Room with its boat-shaped table, so designed in order that every guest can see each other when seated. I was directed to put the box on a thick green baize cloth on the table. We were asked to take a seat to wait for the Prime Minister. We remained quietly chatting and admiring the room and the paintings on the walls.

The Prime Minister entered the room and to my amazement was closely followed by my father – my jaw dropped with surprise. Loader then introduced everyone to the PM but when he got to me, the PM interjected and made a joke about a 'chip off the old block' and turned to my father.

'You have done very well, I understand,' he said with a broad smile, acknowledging me, while my father stood by with great pride. They both shook my hand warmly.

My father quietly said, 'No wonder you didn't answer your damned telephone in Tasmania.'

'No, that's right – I was rather busy,' I said, and we both smiled in a knowing manner.

'Who is the pretty young lady?' he whispered rather admiringly.

'Oh, that's Fiona, my good friend.' He obviously liked her.

The Prime Minister then spoke up. 'Congratulations to all of you. I wonder if I may see these famous pages that have caused you so much trouble.' So saying he inclined his head towards me.

'Yes, of course Prime Minister,' I said, 'although it might be advisable if we could perhaps wait for the two Professors who would give you a very expert opinion and explain to you why they are so valuable.' The PM understood, and nodded in agreement.

I was then asked to lay the pages out on the large curved table with Loader's help, and by the time we had finished Professor Watson-Young and Professor Fitzmaurice had arrived. They took the PM very proudly around the table, describing the finer points of the work. They explained about the many pigments, especially the *Lapis lazuli*, a finely ground semi-precious blue stone from Afghanistan, and other places around the world; and how 'Orpiment' not gold was used in the illumination of *The Book* in those early days. They also explained how these substances were applied to the vellum or parchment. My father followed beside him closely, quietly observing everything.

The Prime Minister expressed great surprise about the Orpiment which was imported from far away Asia Minor. So Professor Fitzmaurice explained that it was arsenic trisulphide, which in its natural substance has a sparkle giving the appearance of metallic gold. This caused the early illuminators a tremendous amount of trouble, because the sulphide content attacks the neighbouring colours. However, the illuminators who worked on the book overcame most of the problems, but not quite all.

Meanwhile Fiona, Captain Stewart and I were offered a pleasant and much needed meal in the small dining room at the rear of the house. Loader eventually joined us and ate his meal hurriedly and told us once again that the PM was pleased.

'We had better get moving, so hurry and finish up,' he said finally, in a rush. Loader was now feeling the pressure because he was taking control again. 'The Professors are going over to Dublin by air with the PM this afternoon,' he explained.

I collected the box which had been re-packed carefully by the Professors. We were thanked once again by the PM as he shook hands at the front door.

The three cars were about to move off at last, when my father had one final word with me before leaving, indicating he was especially pleased, which was most unlike him because he was usually most restrained in his dry manner.

The four of us settled back comfortably in the car, with Loader skilfully taking us through London in a northerly direction and getting on to the M1 Motorway. We circumnavigated Coventry and Birmingham and on to North Wales. South of Manchester on the M56 the traffic was intense and slowed us up considerably, but we joined the road to Bangor and eventually crossed the Menai Strait Bridge to the Isle of Anglesey.

By now the traffic was lighter, and as I watched Loader out of the corner of my eye, I saw he was plainly exhausted, so I said, 'Would you like me to take over?' Because we had an uneventful run with no dramas, we had relaxed slightly and Fiona had dozed off occasionally, I noticed.

'No, we are nearly there thanks – not worth it, only another half hour,' he said politely.

Finally we reached Holyhead, and Victoria Road and the car ferry loading ramp. We were slightly late and the ferry had been held back especially for us and our important cargo, which of course the fare-paying passengers could not be made aware of.

We were the last vehicle on and they watched us in sullen silence, obviously not at all pleased. No explanation was given by the Captain or crew for security reasons. We were almost safely there – or so we thought.

The two police cars returned to London; we thanked them cordially for their help. The journey up to this point was uneventful and had lulled me into a false sense of security. We were escorted up to the bridge and the Captain's cabin.

Some discussion took place about where to put the box for maximum safety. So with the Captain's agreement, we placed it in his overnight safe where we could keep a close eye on it. The Captain informed us that the crossing normally took three and a half hours, but this time would be longer because we were starting late. We made ourselves comfortable in the small lounge, but the Captain took pity on Fiona and made a temporary bed for her in his cabin.

After a while I left the bridge and went downstairs for a snack, leaving Loader in charge with Captain Stewart, with the intention of changing guard in due course.

It was when I was returning to the bridge that something happened that was unexpected. We were about half way across the Irish Sea, when a large cabin cruiser came towards us and deliberately cut across our bows, swerved around us and circled around the stern of the ferry. We could see two gunmen on the deck of the cruiser firing accurately upwards at the bridge, and with a loud hailer ordering the Captain to heave-to immediately.

I managed to gain the relative safety of the bridge while the cabin cruiser was on the other side of the ferry. As I stepped in, the scene before me was chaotic; everyone was flat on the floor, which was littered with shards of glass, chunks of metal and plastic. The Captain, who had obviously seen the cabin cruiser coming first, had shouted a warning and was still at his post in charge. He ordered an increase in speed which brought another burst of gunfire.

The Captain was hit and more bits of the bridge structure flew everywhere. Loader managed to struggle onto his knees and crawled over to the Captain, who was on the floor bleeding severely from a shoulder wound, and ordered him to heave-to at once. The Second in Command took charge temporarily and brought the ferry under control.

When we came to a stop, the gunmen boarded swiftly, and with another burst of gunfire charged into the wheelhouse and aggressively demanded the wooden box. They were both masked and their clothing was plain gray and indistinct. Loader and I knew immediately who they were.

Loader turned to me and said, 'Give them the box please, would you Jack?'

'Not bloody likely, after all the trouble I've been through to get it,' I said through my teeth. My jaw tightened in surprise as Loader drew a gun on me. I measured the distance between the two of us and realised I couldn't disarm him before he got a shot off. I opened the safe reluctantly and took out the box with as much bad grace as I could gather.

'You bloody bastard!' I shouted in fury again, although I also sensed that he was acting rather strangely.

'Do as I ask please, Jack. I won't ask again,' he shouted back angrily, pointing the gun at me.

I realised I had no choice, so I picked up the box with fury and gave it to the nearest gunman, while the second gunman kept us covered. They quickly left after making an obscene gesture.

There followed an awkward silence and I stared at Loader, stunned and amazed. 'How could you, you damned fool?' I shouted. As he pocketed the gun and put on the safety catch, he just smiled and said quietly, 'We were just the decoy Jack. The real pages went with the PM and the Professors by air this afternoon under armed guard, of course. The swap was made at Number 10 while you and Fiona were eating.'

Once again, he had out-manoeuvred the crooks and me, so I said, 'What about the dangers of travelling by air with the pages to Dublin? Thought that was inadvisable?'

'The Professors had a serious re-think about this and relented about their decision. You understand, for such a short flight, they thought the risk worth taking.'

The Captain was then helped onto his feet and swiftly attended to. Fiona was checked over too, with a sprained wrist which happened when the first burst of gunfire came crashing through the bridge, the ferry rolled slightly and she fell onto the hard floor, half asleep.

'Sorry about the deception Jack. I'd rather you were a live coward than a dead hero,' Loader muttered softly.

'Thanks for that, at least,' I said thoughtfully.

I was still fuming as much from being tricked as handing over the box. I went over to Fiona, who had recovered quickly from the shock.

The intercom crackled and asked for any doctors to, 'Please come up to the bridge.' The Captain, although shaken and slightly wounded, now felt strong enough to take charge and was concerned that some passengers might be badly injured or worse. Doctors and nurses arrived on the bridge within minutes. They were given instructions, then dispersed among the passengers.

Loader stood to the right of the Captain with a powerful pair of binoculars, searching for the large cabin cruiser which had quickly disappeared somewhere into the misty Irish Sea. The radar had received an unlucky hit too, which made it inoperable, but the Radar Officer assured us it was no problem. 'We could find our way to the Irish Coast by compass – just steer due West,' he said confidently, 'till we reach the coast.'

I spoke to the Captain and Loader as they scanned the horizon. 'Which direction did they go?' thinking out loud.

'Not sure,' came Loader's reply, 'and there was no name on the boat, it had been skilfully painted over.'

'What about the voice that hailed us to heave to? What sort of accent did it have?' I said rather hopefully.

'That's an interesting question,' said Loader, 'I thought it was American or possibly Irish.'

'More American I think,' said the Captain, who had a better knowledge of the different Irish accents.

'Navigation chart, someone,' ordered the Captain. The chart appeared almost instantly and was placed on the big table as we gathered round. He put his finger on the chart. 'Right, we were about here when hi-jacked, and we have hardly moved since. Do you realise the hijackers could be making for anywhere? We are within easy reach of the North Coast of England, Northern Ireland, Eire, West Coast of Wales, West Scotland or even the Isle of Man. Although I think that's most unlikely,' he said, pointing out the different ports of interest on the map.

The sea mist was now becoming a problem and the daylight was fading rapidly. All navigation lights were on, as were the foghorns to give a warning. We proceeded at half speed for safety, and eventually were greeted by another boat – an Irish naval one this time thankfully, although we weren't sure at first. The gunmen might be returning if they opened the box early and found out what was really in it. Loader told me later it was a copy of the London Times, carefully cut and folded to fit, then locked and covered in plastic bubblewrap. I realised Loader's thorough planning had worked once again.

We were thankful when the naval boat came alongside and the crew came aboard to see what kind of help we needed. They radioed a report back to Dublin. The naval boat then guided us into Dublin Ferry Terminal. Every light in the City of Dublin seemed to be on to help us into the harbour. The cars and passengers were escorted off by the crew with extreme courtesy and ambulances were standing by on the dockside to attend to the wounded. Thankfully, there were very few needed.

I turned to Loader and said without spite: 'Were there any bullets in that gun?'

'Yes, fully loaded. But not for you – for them if necessary,' he said smiling.

My mouth dropped slightly. 'You were taking a terrible great risk. I suppose I should have spotted it when you said 'please'. Not once, but twice! You never say please, do you?'

He didn't answer but just pulled a strange funny face. It could have been a bloodbath if he had been wrong.

Fiona, Loader and Captain Stewart joined me at the rail as we watched the cars disappear into the night. I put my arm around Fiona in a protective manner, and to keep her warm, and she said, 'What a day to remember! I'm hoping for a nice comfortable hotel bed tonight.'

'We deserve the best,' I said, and sure enough it was the most comfortable bed I had ever slept in. I awoke the next morning fully refreshed and hoping to see as much of Dublin and the *Book of Kells* as possible now that the danger was over, or so I believed. The ceremony of handing over the missing pages would also be a wonderful culmination to my quest.

I stared out of the hotel room window and in the front of the hotel was a large cluster of the world's press waiting to interview someone, or indeed anyone, who would give them further details about the event in the Irish Sea. It was their job I realised, but it was not my position to give any statements or interviews about the events. They knew something serious had happened, possibly by following us to the hotel. Putting two and two together they had come up with only half the story.

The furious knocking on our door was loud and insistent, so I indicated for Fiona to hide for safety and I answered the door very cautiously. Thankfully it was the hotel manager who came in and spoke quietly, while handing me both Irish and British newspapers. He also advised us to call him on the hotel phone, so that he could get us out by a secure exit if we wanted to leave the hotel and avoid the press.

We sat down to study the very large headlines which said 'Holyhead to Dublin Ferry High-jacked by Gunmen', giving some details of the hold-up by a mystery cabin cruiser from 'out of the blue.' Where they got the information from was difficult to assess but most of it was correct. Fortunately there was no mention of our wooden box, or its contents. I assumed Loader and Captain Stewart were equally informed, so I rang Loader in his room.

'Have you seen the newspapers?' I said.

'Yes, I have,' he said in a rush. 'I advise total silence from all of us, it's not our job to talk to the press.'

'I agree. They won't connect our project with the ferry boat hijacking will they? Thank goodness the Prime Minister's party went by air.'

'Yes, by the way, I have three invitations to the afternoon ceremony for you both, and Captain Stewart.'

He put the phone down before I could ask him my next question, so my first question when we all met in his room was, 'How did they know we were crossing from Holyhead to Dublin?'

'Well', he started thoughtfully,' they must have seen us somehow outside No. 10, as there is always a crowd of people outside, and followed us at a distance to Holyhead and obviously worked out our planned route to Dublin. Either that, or we have a mole in our midst.'

There was an unpleasant hush as we looked at each other in surprise. I broke the silence. 'Loader! I don't think that's possible,' I shouted, 'that's absolute rubbish, if you think about it carefully. How could any of us contact them? We have been together all of the time!'

'I'm only thinking out loud. Yes, of course you're right,' he replied. 'Sorry, very bad joke.'

'I have thought many times,' I said angrily, 'throughout my long quest, how is it they have managed to follow me so closely and the answer I always came up with was the massive amount of manpower at their disposal, and that can only mean lots of money,' I said thoughtfully.

'Meaning that whoever put up the money is obscenely rich?' interjected Captain Stewart. 'Obviously, a billionaire at the very least.'

'Yes, a dishonest and desperate one. That last attempt on the ferry boat was the action of a very angry man. He was probably at the wheel of the cabin cruiser himself, his employees having failed to get what he wanted. He probably made the final attempt himself,' said Loader.

I was still sore about Loader's deception, so I asked him why he didn't let me in on the secret. His answer was, 'If I had told you, how would you have reacted?'

'Oh, I see – probably very differently. I might have handed it over without protest,' I replied.

'Exactly!' was the emphatic reply, with a knowing look on his face.

'But how did you know they would try that?'

'I didn't, it was just a strong possibility. I had a back-up plan, and was well prepared. I was right wasn't I? Hence my gun was loaded and ready,' he said.

'You sneaky old fox,' I said. I slowly shook my head in disbelief. 'But you were quite correct.'

'Right! Now if there aren't any more questions, here are your special invitations for the ceremony,' he replied, as he handed them to us. We thanked him, and Fiona and I retired to our room to recuperate and smarten ourselves up for the ceremony. Before leaving Loader's room however, he had a final quiet word with me saying, 'I did choose the right man for the job, didn't I?'

'I like to think so,' I replied quietly, with grin.

'Although I had my doubts at times,' he said smiling. He put his arm around my shoulder and shook my hand, and then kissed Fiona.

His action was such a surprise to us because of his usual qualities of restraint, determination and calm planning which seemed to have gone out of the window. He had triumphed, but so had Fiona and I; and Captain Stewart too.

We all attended the ceremony in the afternoon. Loader sat in the front row with other dignitaries including the Prime Ministers. Fiona and I sat with Captain Stewart further back in the body of the hall. My father sat to the right of the British Prime Minister, looking very pleased.

The ceremony started with a rousing selection of Irish and British music and the Prime Ministers were introduced by the local compere. The Irish PM gave a short speech of welcome to his British counterpart, who then gave a very brief history of the search for the missing pages, obviously written by Loader, but missing out the detailed secret parts concerning the deserted village of Imber on Salisbury Plain.

He received thanks and everyone politely applauded and then cheered. The orchestra finished the stately occasion with some lively Irish music, performed by a young red-haired beauty who was the lead violinist.

The compere then invited members of the audience to take this once in a lifetime opportunity to view the lost pages for the first time, which took them over two hours. Their fascination was clearly obvious. The pages had been placed in a temporary glass display case for protection.

The National Irish Press had a field day, and the next day the return of the lost pages was headlines, saying: 'Incredibly Valuable Historic Treasure – Found.'

At last we could relax, so Fiona and I took Captain Stewart for a stroll around Dublin's sights and finished up in one of their charming old pubs, which was crowded with friendly local revellers and filled with historic charm and atmosphere.

ISLAND HOLIDAY

The next day we said goodbye to Captain Stewart, who returned to his wife in London. What a story he had to tell her! Fiona and I returned to the East Pavilion of the Colonnades Library to see the *Book of Kells*, the Book of Armagh 807AD and the *Book of Durrow* written in 675AD, which is even earlier than the *Book of Kells*. I had kept my promise to Father Kelly in the Vatican Library and would confirm it all in writing, later.

It had been an adventure for us both and as Fiona seemed so relaxed and cheerful, I asked her again about visiting Tasmania. This time I received a more positive answer, but she had one additional proposal.

'And what would that be?' I asked, with a worried smile.

'That we go to Cornwall first and the Isles of Scilly,' she replied with a smile. 'For a week's holiday. I've always wanted to go there with someone special, and I think you fit the bill.'

And that's what we did, calling in to Wiltshire on the way to say a big 'thank you' personally to the Reverend Paul Charlton, the Matron, and also to settle up financially with my friend Dick Cooper near Salisbury over the loss of his old Austin 1800.

It was towards the end of our much deserved holiday that I received a phone call from Loader in London. He informed me that the Department had now rounded up all our protagonists and from the information collected, it was an American banker who was the mastermind behind our troubles.

He was originally a politician who resigned with a fortune and joined the banking world and Wall Street.

'I thought there was a lot of money behind it somewhere,' I said sarcastically. 'He obviously had no scruples at all. Can I ask his name?'

'No, definitely not,' said Loader emphatically.

'What happens next?' I inquired.

'Nothing as far as you are concerned. The American authorities are keeping a very close eye on him. I will let you know if there are any developments. Enjoy your holiday and regards to Fiona.'

And so saying he put down the phone.

Finis

Acknowledgements

This book had its genesis years ago and therefore there are many people who I would like to thank for either help or encouragement.

First I would like to thank my wife and family, our daughter Julia who took a great interest in my efforts and typed up the first chapter so that I could see it in print. Our family friend Bronwen Watkins who typed it again with appropriate improvements.

Thank you to the three experienced calligraphers who advised me: first, my wife June who also did the design for the cover and the illustrations; good friends Gemma Black (Canberra and Tasmania) and Helen Warren (Sydney).

To The Eastern Shore Writers' Group and Marion Stoneman for their continuing support, my heartfelt thanks.

Dear long-time friends Janet and Frank Scrivener for assistance in taking some excellent photographs of St Mary's Church, Market Lavington in Wiltshire, that helped me visualise an important segment in the story.

A big thank you to Pat Lloyd who pulled my handwritten scribbling into a well organised format.

And finally, thank you to Sheelagh Wegman my accredited editor for essential final corrections that are so important, and to the many friends who encouraged me – your kind words kept me working and on the right track to complete the book.

Thank you.

I accept full responsibility for any historical and scientific anomalies that may appear in the story.

Roger D. Francis

Glossary of Terms

VELLUM: Parchment from calf, sheep or goat skin, prepared for writing on.

LIMNER: A person (usually a monk or nun) trained in the ruling of lines on vellum, showing a faint indentation for a scribe to follow to keep the writing straight.

SCRIBE: A person trained in the ancient art of calligraphy and beautiful writing.

ILLUMINATION: The art of decoration in manuscripts, including colours and gold.

SCRIPTORIUM: A room in a building (a monastery or other) where books are created and stored.

MANUSCRIPT: A group of pages containing words; a book.

ABBOT: A religious man appointed to an elevated position in holy orders; a person in authority over monks or nuns in an abbey or monastery.

BROTHERS: The collective name given to men in holy orders in a monastery.

HALF UNCIAL: Book script in common use between the 5th & 8th centuries with ascenders and descenders.

INSULAR UNCIAL: A style of capital letters indicating their origin was from the Irish-British Isles' style used in the 7th and 8th centuries.

The Author

R oger D. Francis was born in Southern England. His background is in architecture, art and design. In his teens he was keenly interested in Roman archaeology, which has led to a lifelong interest in history, old documents and ancient maps. He is now living in Tasmania Australia with his wife, and family.

Printed in Australia
AUOC02n1128170214
259839AU00004B/4/P